All for One
Love, War, & Ghosts

Professional Review

McGuinn explores the legacy and costs of war that veterans carry long after their service, and the concepts of loyalty and duty to friends, as well as potential life paths not taken. The shift in tone from light-hearted to the very serious topics at the end is unexpected, but works in a very thematic form of storytelling.

Written in a plainspoken, accessible tone, *All For One* is an easy read... While her writing makes sparse use of metaphor or lyrical imagery, McGuinn's words carry emotional resonance in the small details that serve to highlight the trauma of war, loss, and love without overstating these feelings... McGuinn writes her characters with an eye for realism rather than according to an archetype.

These are selected comments written by a *Publishers Weekly* reviewer as part of the critical assessment the BookLife Prize provides for each entrant. The full report may be accessed on the author's BookLife profile:

https://booklife.com/project/all-for-one-love-war-ghosts-102070

Some reviews from readers:

What starts off like a gentle little YA read with hometown kids bonding, growing up together, crushes, breakups, the boys going off to service together...much the way anyone growing up in the 50s/60s would relate to, ends with a heart-wrenching experience of the aftermath of war, PTSD, love, death, abandonment, grief, and revenge that take a toll on the returning warriors and all who love them. Masterfully written with suspense at every turn. The style is very personable, allowing us to jump right into the families, their inner workings, joys, conflicts as if we were there at the family dinner tables, part of the clan.
Jo Lauer, author *****

I am not normally a fiction reader, I prefer non-fiction. If this book hadn't been put in front of me, I would not have found it nor have made the choice to read it. This fiction story, however, has real-world relatability - to the past and present - and suspense in the right places. I couldn't put it down and it was a fast read.
Heather Guido: *****

In its first pages, this realistic historical novel took me back to my own high school years, when the Vietnam War was vividly waged on TV every night and bubbled up in every conversation. The saga moves forward in time a half century, the characters on the edge of retirement, and yet they remain haunted by their 'Nam experiences. As the modern mystery unfolds, readers are reminded how wars, official or otherwise, damage the human spirit, a very timely read and one that will keep the reader pondering the story long afterwards.
Joan M. Griffin****

This story reminds me of the kids I knew that went to Vietnam. The twist makes it readable. Good story.
Chris Cameron: ****

All for One
Love, War, & Ghosts

Sheri McGuinn

Durare
Publishing

Bullhead City, AZ

This book is a work of fiction. Real locales and events have been used fictitiously. Each character is a composite of multiple moments with multiple people, blended with a hefty dose of the author's imagination. None of them should be considered representative of any real event or real person, living or dead.

www.sherimcguinn.com

smcguinn@sherimcguinn.com

sherimcguinn.substack.com

Copyright 2025

978-1-942069-10-2 Pbk

978-1-942069-11-9 Kindle

Library of Congress Control Number: 2025911116

Cover Design by Sheri McGuinn

Boots & photograph images licensed through Shutterstock.

HUMAN AUTHORED
Authors Guild
5164749

Table of Contents

RESOURCES

THANK YOU

BEHIND THE STORY

ACKNOWLEDGMENTS

ALSO BY SHERI MCGUINN

DISCUSSION QUESTIONS

To those who serve and those who love them.

Ancient History

Time plays games on us as we age. Events that are ancient history, moments that altered the course of our lives, seem to have happened yesterday. People and times we thought we left behind have immense importance later in our journeys. Decisions made with youthful certainty come back to haunt us

The Musketeers

Through the nineteen fifties and sixties, three boys grew up together in a small town that could have been anywhere in the United States. It could have been your town. The boys could have been your friends.

Everyone, even teachers and parents, called the three boys the Musketeers because they always did everything together. Janet, a sword-fighting tomboy when they were little and a good sport as they became teens, was an honorary fourth Musketeer.

Cathy, the girl next door to Janet, was a year behind them. The two girls played together as toddlers, but when Janet's mother gave her more freedom to go play in the park across the street without direct supervision, Janet discovered it was much more fun to play with the boys than have tea parties with Cathy. On rare occasions the younger girl was included as a damsel in distress. The two girls remained friends as they got older. They just didn't spend very much time together, especially when the Musketeers moved up to high school a year ahead of Cathy.

So it was, at the end of one beautiful fall day Cathy's freshman year, the two girls were chatting in the hallway when the three Musketeers came jostling their way toward the exit. Rob was in the lead, as usual, but when he saw Cathy he stopped and stared, mouth open, as if he'd never seen her before. Henry and Dave continued on toward the front door, calling back for Janet to join them. "We're heading to the Tastee Freeze."

Rob tore his gaze away from Cathy and followed his friends, but turned back to say, "Janet, bring your friend."

His smile warmed Cathy from the inside out, and she returned it timidly.

Soon the group of four became five friends who did everything together. Instead of sword fights, there were movies and bowling and bonfires at the beach.

A few weeks after that first ice cream came a party at the lake. Cathy joined the circle around a spinning bottle, hoping it might point to Rob when she spun it. Instead, a pimply-faced boy she barely knew gave her a slobbery smack on the lips. Cathy pulled away as if bitten. When the boy laughed and asked if that was her first kiss, anyone could see it had been. But she gave pretending it wasn't a valiant try.

She wiped her hand across her mouth and shook it as if to get rid of excessive slobber, gave the boy a withering look, got up, and walked down the beach away from the gathering.

Rob had felt a strange contraction in his chest when that boy kissed Cathy. He found himself following her away from the party, taking her hand in his without a word, just a quick gentle squeeze. They walked hand in hand all the way to the point, far from the bonfire, until they could go no further. He turned to face Cathy, still with that odd feeling in his chest. They stared into each other's eyes for long moments, then he leaned forward to kiss her, gently exploring Cathy's lips and mouth with the tip of his tongue until she responded in kind.

The next three years, most of their dates included the other Musketeers and Janet, but everyone recognized Rob and Cathy as a couple. When Rob got a worse-for-wear old Ford Falcon, Cathy would squeeze up against him as he drove while Janet sat on her other side and Henry and Dave rode in the back. The girls had decided on this seating arrangement, because a girl in the back seat with two boys would have the town gossips deciding she did it with both of them.

Janet stopped hanging out with the Musketeers part way through their senior year, hoping the boy she was crushing on would notice her. When he invited someone else to prom,

Janet reclaimed her spot in the group and they all went together—though Rob and Cathy ended up crowned king and queen.

They were everyone's favorite couple. In the almost three years they'd been together, they'd never had the tiffs and break-ups other teenage couples had.

Sometimes Rob got upset about current events, but Cathy blocked out most of that unpleasantness or diverted his attention. Kissing him usually worked.

Then the middle of May, Rob took Cathy for a walk by the lake and told her she should date other people and have fun her senior year of high school. At first she thought he was just being gallant and didn't really mean it.

She stopped and faced him. "I love you. I don't want to date anyone else."

He shook off her hand. "I'm leaving. One way or another. Who knows what's going to happen. Don't sit around waiting for me." He turned away and moved quickly back toward his car, sure he was doing the best thing for her.

Cathy's heart shattered. She didn't connect this to the news from Ohio that had upset him. She'd already put that out of her mind. She thought this meant he wanted to date other girls at college.

Tears poured down her face as she watched him leave her. She'd never said the words before, neither of them had, but she'd been so sure they felt the same way about each other.

July 1, 1970

The only way to avoid Rob was to avoid the Musketeers altogether. Cathy didn't go to their graduation or any of the parties that followed. She sat home alone, not leaving the house for days in a row.

On the first of July she looked out her bedroom window and saw Janet standing by the curb, clearly waiting for the guys to pick her up. *I'm going to be alone the rest of my life. I miss all of them.* Cathy blinked to stop her tears, got a tissue from her dresser, and blew her nose. *Enough feeling sorry for myself.*

She hurriedly rinsed her face and rushed out to join Janet. "Hey, what do you guys have planned for the holiday?"

"Nothing's set yet." Janet looked up the street instead of at Cathy. "We want to get through today first."

"What's today?"

"The lottery. We're going to listen on the car radio." Janet hugged herself.

"Why? The guys don't have to worry about that until next year." Why waste a beautiful summer day listening to names being drawn for the draft?

"Henry's older. They held him back so he could be with his friends." Janet grimaced. "His birthday is July 9th. I hope he gets number 300 or something."

A cold rock settled in Cathy's stomach. In eighth grade she'd been required to discuss the news each day. It was supposed to build a habit for conscientious citizenship. A vision of those nightly clips from Vietnam came to her now—dead and maimed bodies, brought from battle on helicopters, complete with the daily body count as if they were keeping score.

She had avoided current events ever since, kept it distant. Now it was too close. "Henry's my friend, too. You all are. I should be there."

Janet shrugged. "I don't know if there'll be room. Dave's kid brother Steve has been riding along with us sometimes."

At least he wasn't a new girlfriend for Rob. "He's like a seventh grader, isn't he?"

"Eighth next year. Dave doesn't let him drink."

Just then Rob pulled up. Dave and Henry flanked a cooler in the back. The front seat was open.

"Cathy's coming." Janet's voice didn't invite argument. She slid across the front seat to the middle position.

The boys in the back exchanged friendly greetings with Cathy as she got in beside Janet and closed the door. Rob remained silent as he drove them out of town. Empty cups still blew across the field where they parked, reminders of weeks of graduation parties. They rolled down the windows as Rob monkeyed with the car radio.

Cathy pictured him kissing other girls, then gave herself a little shake. *We're here for Henry. A lottery—they're gambling with his life.*

Janet reached a hand over her head. "Pass up a Coke, would you?"

Henry pulled one out of the cooler and passed her the dripping can without his normal razzing about her never drinking. He popped the tab on a beer and chugged the entire can. He let out a long belch before announcing his decision. "If it looks like I'll get drafted for sure, I'll go enlist right away." He tried to look cool by crushing his beer can, but his jaw clenched and his Adam's apple bobbed as he swallowed hard.

Dave's voice cracked as he said, "You could still get a student deferment."

"Yeah, but if my number is low, I'd have to go as soon as I'm done with college. I'd have that hanging over me for four years." Henry shook his head.

"Quiet," Rob ordered. "I've got it coming in now. They're drawing birthdates from one drum and the draft placement from another."

They listened quietly through the first ten pairs.

The eleventh draw changed everything.

" July 9th... Zero, zero, one."

Rob snapped off the radio.

For a moment, there was absolute silence.

"Shit." Henry got out of the car and leaned over to puke, hands on his thighs.

In the car, Rob turned to Dave. "You still in?"

The blood had drained from Dave's face. He pushed his hair back, gripping his head in his hands and displaying the scar he normally kept hidden, reminder of a bike accident when they were twelve. He took a breath, let it out slowly, lowered his hands, and nodded.

Cathy stared at Rob's profile, her heart pushing up into her throat.

Janet's head swiveled between Rob and Dave. "What are you talking about?"

Rob glanced over his shoulder as he opened his door, but didn't make eye contact with either of the girls. "Wait in the car."

Cathy's throat closed. She screamed silently as she watched the two boys approach their friend on either side, each putting a hand on his shoulder. Henry looked up at them with terror in his eyes. He wiped his mouth with the back of his hand.

"Three Musketeers, man," squeaked Dave, his voice tight with tension.

Rob nodded. "All for one, one for all... I checked into it. We can go in on the buddy system, go through basic training together, and maybe on beyond that."

No! Drive him to Canada! Anything but this! But Cathy couldn't make a sound.

Letters

Cathy didn't watch the news. She only read the funnies and Ann Landers in the newspaper. But crystal clear images of boys on stretchers remained. She was terrified her friends might end up on stretchers in Vietnam.

After they enlisted, she began paying attention to current events. As soon as she read about troops being reduced, she ran over to Janet's house to share the good news.

Henry's mom was sitting at the kitchen table, sobbing. Janet's mom was rubbing her arm, trying to console her.

Janet pulled stunned Cathy back outside and away from the house. "They're all being deployed to Vietnam as soon as their basic training is finished."

"Why? The troops are being reduced! The President said so!"

Janet shook her head. "They've been saying that for at least a year, before Nixon announced we were invading Cambodia, before the National Guard gunned down those students at Kent State. Why would you believe anything the government says?"

Cathy vaguely remembered Rob being angry about things on the news shortly before they broke up, but as always, she'd blocked out the unpleasantness. "I wish they'd all gone to Canada."

Cathy wrote to each of the boys every week without fail. Rob wrote back once, while they were still in training, to tell her he'd decided to be a medic, to save as many lives as he could. He again encouraged her to date and have fun—but also warned her to be careful when she started college, to stay away from demonstrations and any military or police response on campus.

Henry was the only one who wrote back once they were all in Vietnam.

Dear Cathy,

Thanks for writing. I'm wishing I'd gotten around to having a steady girlfriend now. But I guess it wouldn't be fair to expect a girl to sit at home not knowing if I'd even make it back. And Dear John letters are hard to take here. It's nice to have you writing, though.

I'm doing okay so far, but Dave's having a hard time. Rob and his "All for one" crap—and then he went and ditched us to be a medic. I was going to end up here, but Dave didn't have to. I'm not sure you knew, but his father died when we were in grade school so his mom's on her own with Stevie. He's in eighth grade this year and Dave's all kinds of worried about him, too. If you could check up on him, let me know and I'll tell Dave how he's doing.

I'm so PO'd about Rob. Sorry for the language, but I'm really mad. I can't tell you much about what we're doing or where we are. It's raining. I'll try to find other stuff to write about, but I've got to finish up for now. Mail's going out.

Yours truly, Henry

Henry wrote every week, talking mostly about the rain. Then there were weeks without letters. Cathy kept writing, hoping he was okay. When she finally saw an envelope with the red and blue edging, she could breathe easily again.

Dear Cathy,

I got malaria and they sent me out to a hospital. Sorry I didn't write, but my temp was up and it probably wouldn't have made much sense. Feeling much better now and I'm back with the unit. Dave's still here. Guess it was pretty rough while I was out. But I think he'll be okay. Knowing Stevie's staying out of trouble helps. Thanks for that.

I finally read the letters you sent while I was sick. I still get tired kind of quick, so I'll sign off now. Thanks for writing.

Yours Truly, Henry

The next week, Janet told Cathy that Dave had been killed. His dog tags were all that came home.

Homecomings

Henry's first tour ended two months after they heard about Dave.

He surprised everyone by volunteering to go back. Cathy arranged to come home from college the last weekend he was on leave. They spent all day Saturday with Janet, visiting childhood haunts, talking about the good old days. They were walking on the beach at sunset when conversation turned to plans for the future.

Janet declared that she was going to get as far away as possible, once she completed her business program. "One more year and that's it—I'm out of here! I'm going to move to a city where people don't think they know everything about me and I'll never come back."

Cathy picked up a piece of shale and skipped it across the water—a triple. "I think I'll come home to teach, once I get my degree and certification."

"Me too." Henry threw a piece of shale, but it sank. "Not teaching, but, assuming I make it home again, I don't ever want to leave."

Janet glared at him. "So why are you going back now?"

Henry stared out over the water. His body slumped as he exhaled. "I have to." He inhaled deeply. He could never let anyone know what he'd done. "I... there're things I need to do."

He turned and faced the girls. He searched for an explanation they could accept. Something he was doing right. "Like, there's this kid, an orphan, living on the street, with one eye. He lost the other to shrapnel. I've been making sure he gets enough to eat."

"But will you even be near him when you go back?" Cathy took his hand and held his gaze. "It makes no sense."

Henry blushed at the touch. "There'll probably be someone else I can help. Besides, they really are cutting back on troops now and I know what I'm doing. It's better for me to go back than let some green kid replace me. They'd probably be shot the first day."

Cathy wanted to yell at him that she didn't want to lose any more friends. But she held her tongue because it was too late to change anything.

Sunday, Henry volunteered to drive her back to college in his rental car.

She showed him her room and the campus, then walked him back to the parking lot. "Thanks for the ride. My dad really didn't want to make the trip twice in one weekend."

"Thanks for coming home to see me." Henry took her hand as they stood face-to-face. "I really appreciate it, and all the letters you send. They usually come in a batch, but I read one each day to make it last."

Cathy blushed a little. "I like getting your letters, too."

Henry bent to give her a chaste kiss on the mouth, then got into the car and rolled down his window to say goodbye.

"Come back safe." Cathy leaned into the car to return his kiss, then stood and waved until the car turned a corner and was gone.

Later that week, Cathy found Rob sitting on her bed in her dorm room when she got back from class. She stopped in the doorway.

"Your roommate let me in, then she left to do laundry." He didn't get up.

Cathy walked across the room and put her books on her desk. "How did you know where to find me?"

"I got your letters. Eventually. Mail's not that regular over there."

Cathy leaned back against the desk, facing him. "You didn't write back."

Rob rocked slightly, his fingertips tense against each other. "Have you been dating? You didn't say."

"Some. Are you home for good?" She turned her back on him and tidied her already tidy desk.

"I want to be, but they need medics on the choppers. I'll probably stay over there until my active service is done. I'd go nuts dealing with military stupidity here anyway."

She blinked to stop unwanted tears. "Henry's going back, too."

"Because he wants to." Rob spit the words out, then sighed. "We had a fight about it."

Cathy turned around and faced him again, her eyes glistening but her cheeks still dry. "You saw him?"

"Yeah, he said you kissed him." Rob looked miserable.

Cathy lifted her chin. "Just a peck. We're friends."

"He didn't take it that way."

"Well, that's what it was, and even if it wasn't, what business is it of yours?" Cathy took two steps forward with an accusing finger pointed at Rob. "*You* broke up with *me*, told me to date other people."

Rob lurched to his feet and Cathy smelled the booze on his breath.

"I didn't mean someone else who might die on you." He reached out and pulled her into his arms, kissed her hair. "I love you, Cath."

He sat down on the bed, bringing Cathy onto his lap.

"Oh, sorry!" The roommate entered and put a basket of laundry on the bed across the room. "Want me to put a sock on the doorknob?" She held up a clean sock.

"No." Cathy eased out of Rob's arms and stood. "We were heading over to the student union. Rob hasn't seen the campus."

She waved for him to follow and headed out the door. He trailed behind.

Once they were outside, she turned on him. "You're only saying you love me because you're drunk and because Henry kissed me. If you want to convince me I'm wrong, tell me when you're sober." She stomped off for the student union without a backward glance.

She didn't see Rob's tears as he stared after her. She stopped writing letters that would never be answered.

Damaged

Cathy and Henry kept writing. She was careful to keep the tone of a friend and he did the same, though his "Truly yours" changed to "Luv you" as the months wore on. When he got back stateside, he was still too far away for visits, or so he said.

Dear Cath,

It's good to be back but the guys who haven't been over there ask stupid questions. There's stuff that happened that I don't ever want to talk about. But it wasn't all like people think, either.

I'm not the same person I was. It's good I'm stationed too far away to come see you. I'm not ready for that yet. I need to be a better person for you.

I should probably not send this, but you need to know what a mess I am.

Luv you, Henry

When he got home for good, Henry came up to her campus for a visit.

He was disappointed, but not surprised, when she told him she had arranged for him to sleep in the boys' dorm. Then she asked about Rob.

Henry's posture stiffened as he spit out the answer. "He's back. Mouthing off against the war and the establishment, whatever he means by that. Looks like a dirty hippie."

He told himself to ease up. *Of course she asked about Rob.*

His tone shifted to genuine concern for his childhood friend. "He's drinking, a lot, smoking pot and I don't know what else. Being a medic did a number on him... Sometimes he starts talking about it... I have to walk away."

The Friday Henry arrived on campus, they went to a party, then a movie and dinner the next day. Cathy avoided holding hands, but at the movie let him put his arm across her seat and rest his hand on her shoulder. When they were standing by his car saying goodbye, he pulled her into his arms for a real kiss, not a friendly peck.

Her body's response pleasantly surprised Cathy. While she had been dating in college, she hadn't felt that spark since Rob—Rob who'd said he loved her but never came back to say it sober.

By the time Cathy came home on break and saw Rob herself, he'd let his hair grow long and greasy. He was drunk or high most of the time and ranting about the Pentagon Papers and how the government lied about everything. He sneered at Henry for volunteering to go kill more people.

Rob came to her house to ask Cathy out, and she said no, not until he pulled himself together. After he left, she cried.

"You did the right thing, Pumpkin." Her father, who'd been in combat in Europe, did not want to see his daughter dealing with a war-damaged man. He gave her a hug. "We always liked Rob, but he needs to work this out himself."

Rob left town to join the protests as a Vietnam Veteran Against the War, though gossip suggested he was headed for a commune. His parents moved to Florida not long after that. He seemed to be gone for good.

The Proposal

Henry settled into a job selling insurance. Cathy went out for a burger with him, then a movie. They kept writing when she went back to college and saw each other on her breaks, then regularly when she graduated and moved home to teach. The relationship grew and deepened. Eventually, the promise of that first kiss was fulfilled.

Janet had ended up living with her parents after they were both disabled in a car accident. If she was seeing someone, they'd double-date with Cathy and Henry. More often, Janet went along as a third wheel. The gossips seemed to see her as a chaperone.

Like any teacher in a small town, Cathy had to be careful of her reputation. She was still living with her parents and never stayed the night at Henry's apartment. Her parents liked Henry, but living with someone was not socially acceptable in their eyes, either. They both pretended to believe she was still a virgin at twenty-four.

Sometimes Cathy could see the war catching up with Henry. He didn't like using his headlights at night. He'd see or hear something that startled him into an alert state or take him from happy to glum in an instant. And he wouldn't talk about anything that happened over there at all. Cathy didn't mention any of that to her father.

Mostly Henry was loving and fun.

One night, he got reservations at the Lakeside Inn. While Cathy was getting ready, her mother came in and suggested she pick a nicer dress.

"The Lakeside's nice, but they don't have a dress code, Mom."

"Please, wear that one you got when you graduated from college."

Cathy capitulated and it was worth it to see Henry's smile when he saw her.

After dinner and dessert, he dropped to one knee there at the table in the restaurant. He held out a small box, opened it to display a diamond ring nestled on velvet-and asked her to marry him.

Her heart pounded, her eyes wide.

I should have known. He asked Dad's permission. That's why Mom insisted on this dress. We've talked about it, as maybe in the future...

She could sense people at nearby tables staring, waiting along with Henry for her answer.

"Yes."

The Wedding

Rob stepped outside the rehearsal hall for some fresh air. Dinner hadn't started and he was already way beyond buzzed.

His AA sponsor had been a long-distance call away this whole month—a month of drinking with old buddies, pretending to be happy. *He'll tell me I should have called anyway. How did I let myself get roped into this?*

He heard two familiar voices drift out from the ladies' room window.

Janet sounded concerned. "What happened to your arm?"

"Darn it. Do you have any concealer?"

"Here. How did you get that bruise?"

"It was an accident. We were watching a movie on Henry's couch. He fell asleep. When it got loud all of a sudden, he startled awake and grabbed my arm. He didn't mean to hurt me. He was having another nightmare about Dave."

Rob's stomach knotted at Cathy's casual tone. He'd cleaned up his act, quit being so angry all the time, started to build a life—and realized he wanted her in it. But he'd waited until he had a year sober before coming back—to find her wedding was already planned.

Henry had asked Rob to be his best man.

Rob knew he should walk away from the window, but he kept listening.

Janet's concern was in her tone. "I thought you said he was getting better…"

Cathy assured her friend, "It's just the stress of the wedding. He'll be fine after that."

"At least your gown has those lace sleeves."

Rob stifled a groan so they wouldn't know he could hear them. Blood pounded in his ears. His body tensed with the urge to rush into the hall and pummel Henry—but tomorrow was Cathy's wedding day.

She'd hate me even more.

Rob's behavior this month certainly didn't reflect the changes he'd made in his life. That first week, he'd tried to convince his friend counseling would really help. Henry had laughed and insisted he just had a bad dream now and then. Rob knew better. That's when he started drinking again. What was the point of being sober when Cathy was going to marry someone way more messed up than he'd ever been?

And Henry had her convinced it was no big deal.

Dammit! She deserves better!

Rob marched into the hall where people were finding their tables for the rehearsal dinner. He spotted Henry laughing in a group and glared at him until the groom finally noticed. Rob nodded toward the double doors with his jaw clenched. He waited until Henry headed his way, then stalked out onto the lawn.

As Henry came outside, Rob turned to face him with hands in fists by his sides.

Henry stopped a few feet back. "You wanted to talk?"

Rob took two steps forward and snarled at Henry. "She deserves better. I should have said something sooner... I should have..."

Henry's face flushed dark red. "You should have what? Huh?" He shoved Rob's chest with both hands.

Rob stumbled back, barely stayed on his feet. Part of his brain registered that he was in no condition to fight.

Words. I have to make him understand. "I – "

But Henry was shouting over him. "I see the way you look at her. Grow up! The prom is ancient history, you two dating was kid stuff. Cathy loves me. I love her."

Rob recognized all of this was true, but he still had to try to protect Cathy. "She shouldn't have to deal with—"

"With what? I have a good job selling insurance. I can take care of her." Henry's lip curled in disgust. "You're the one who's angry at everything. You're the one who turned on and dropped out."

"I'm not the same." Rob's voice broke with anger, pain, and shame. He could feel himself swaying slightly as the three emotions fought for dominance.

"Yeah, right. That act lasted a week. You still drink too much and Rob—you're a lousy, belligerent drunk, always looking for a fight. Cathy was afraid you'd ruin things. She wanted me to choose someone else to be my best man."

Stung, Rob lashed back, meeting Henry's volume. "You don't have any other friends, asshole. It was always just the three of us."

Henry sneered, "Three Musketeers. That was you, always pushing us to do everything together, with you looking cool as the leader. Dave didn't want to enlist. He was scared shitless the whole time—and you left us."

"To be a medic," Rob shouted. At last, he had his balance.

Henry roared, "You have no idea what it was like for us. You didn't see Dave…"

"That's not my fault." Rob crossed his arms. "Dave didn't have to enlist."

"Right." Henry spit out the word and continued shouting. "You talked him into it with your 'All for one, one for all' crap. I had to go, but he didn't. What happened to Dave… that's what gives me nightmares."

"You saw what happened to him and still went back." Rob pulled his crossed arms tight against his chest, instead of taking a swing at Cathy's groom. "But your being screwed up is *my* fault?"

"Yeah."

"Then why ask me to be your best man? While you marry *Cathy*?"

The two men glared at each other until Rob had to blink to stop the tears welling up and threatening to flow.

Henry turned away and exhaled, his shoulders dropping, the fight gone out of him. He spoke quietly. "You're right. I don't have any other friends, not really. I spend my time at work or with Cathy."

Rob dropped his arms. "We've been hanging out with all the guys—"

Henry cut him off. "They're your friends, not mine. You were always friends with everyone. Dave and me? We were just glad you thought we were cool."

The doors burst open and Janet stormed out. "Are you idiots done shouting at each other? Everyone could hear you. Cathy's in tears. She doesn't know if she's having a wedding tomorrow or not."

"Shit." Henry paled as he watched the doors swing shut.

"Yeah, shit." Janet glared at them with arms crossed.

Her stern words had worked. Both men had abandoned their aggressive postures and stared at the building like chastised children.

She eased up with a joke. "You two better not louse up my chance to be maid of honor."

Rob sighed and turned to Henry. "You still want me to be best man tomorrow?"

"Yeah, as long as you know you're not really the best man." Henry half-smiled. "We don't want to ruin Janet's chance to be in a wedding."

Janet gave him a light punch on the arm. "I have a date. I might be a bride someday."

"And it might snow this summer," Rob teased. He turned to Henry. "I'll be there... but I'm done for tonight." He walked away toward the parking lot.

"You're in no condition to drive," Janet called after him.

Rob put up a hand without turning around. "Walking."

Janet pointed at Henry. "You." She waved for him to go inside ahead of her.

The next day, everyone smiled for the wedding photos. Rob slipped away during the reception and didn't come back to town for forty-six years.

July 2022

We never know when time will play its tricks. One moment we can be perfectly content in the present, then the past floods through our lives with the debris of decisions made long ago.

Independence Day Weekend

Friday, July 1, 2022

Cathy looked out the kitchen window at Henry relaxing on his favorite lounge chair, feet up, nursing a chilled Michelob and chatting with their daughter Tina as she set the picnic table.

Tomorrow Tina would be flying overseas to train for her new job. Her ex-husband showed no interest in staying connected to his children, so they'd be with Henry and Cathy for the summer.

Cathy smiled, content with her life.

Lucky for Tina we're in good shape. Way better than my parents were at seventy. Henry's hair may be silver, but it looks good on him. If my roots ever get that light, I may stop being Golden Blonde.

The timer rang for the strawberry-rhubarb pie.

Both strawberries and rhubarb came from their garden, out by the barn and the old orchard. The five acres they'd bought when Tina was a baby had been the homestead of a large farm. At first Cathy, a true townie, had hated the fact she couldn't see a neighbor's house. Now she enjoyed the privacy.

She carried the pie out to the table and stood with her hands on hips, assessing what else was needed. "That's it. We should go get the kids."

Tina bumped shoulders with her mother and raised her eyebrows. "Dad says he's going to give notice this week—says he's retiring."

Cathy's mouth dropped open before she smiled at her husband. "Finally!"

Henry grinned. "You're right, I've got our cushion built up so we're fine and I was thinking, while we have the kids, we should visit some National Parks."

"We'll get to use our senior passes!" Cathy walked over to her husband to give him a peck on the cheek.

Henry continued slyly, "And maybe in the fall, after Tina comes back, we could do one of those European tours you're always talking about. I'd kind of like to visit Ireland."

Cathy hugged him, breathing in his scent—sweetened by a touch of coconut sunscreen. "I'd curl up on your lap right now, but that rickety chair would probably collapse."

An old Kia Rio turned into the long driveway, kicking up dust as it approached. Cathy squinted toward the vehicle. "That's Janet's car. Is she alone?"

"Looks like it," said Tina. "I thought she was with someone now."

Cathy grimaced. "She was, and they were so good together! But Kevin dumped her for a younger woman."

"*Much* younger." Henry got up from the lounge chair, stretching joints he'd kept in one position too long.

They all walked over to Janet's car while she opened the hatch and pulled out a large bowl. "I made the potato salad with eggs, the way you like it, Henry."

"Thanks." He took the bowl. "Hey, I'm retiring—going to give notice next week. Tell Steve I'll be up to review my retirement accounts."

"Glad to hear it. But he's pretty busy the next two weeks. Maybe mid-month?" Janet grabbed a wooden serving spoon and closed the hatch.

"Okay. It's not urgent." Henry carried the potato salad to the table.

Cathy put an arm around her friend. "How are you doing?"

Janet tilted her head with a half-smile. "Same as always." She turned to Cathy's daughter. "Tina, good to see you. Where are the kids?"

"Down at the creek. We were about to go get them. You want to come along?"

"Absolutely. I could use a walk before we eat. I sit way too much now that I'm working for Steve. It's full time until I straighten out the mess his last assistant left behind. Then I can back off on the hours."

Henry had already dished up some potato salad. He took a bite and gave a thumbs-up. "I'll stay here and get the grill going."

As Henry watched the women walk away, he gave silent thanks for his good fortune. The date had not escaped his notice. *Fifty-two years ago. All for one, one for all. It was my number and here I am the one with everything.* He turned on the gas grill to warm up and went into the house for the meat.

Halfway down the driveway, Tina decided to jog ahead. "I have a long plane ride tomorrow. I need a little more exercise."

The older women waved her on.

"Your daughter's living the life I wanted. Flying off across the world." Janet sighed.

Cathy kicked a stone to the side of the driveway. "Is your mom adjusting to her new home?"

"I think so. She doesn't recognize me half the time. And she keeps looking for Dad—doesn't realize he's gone."

"Then there's no reason you can't travel now."

Janet gave a faux laugh. "Except money. Kevin had talked about our traveling, so I looked at tours yesterday. Most of them charge extra for singles."

Cathy gave her a hug. "I'm so sorry about Kevin. You seemed like a good match."

"Seventy and still getting dumped for younger women." Janet shrugged as if it didn't hurt, then changed the topic. "You know Rob's back in town? He bought the building where the bakery used to be and moved in three weeks ago. He's using the downstairs for a photography studio and living in the apartment upstairs."

"I know. I saw his picture on a flyer for his opening."

"Does Henry know? He must have seen those flyers."

"You'd think so." Cathy forced a smile. "I've been waiting for him to say something."

"Maybe he missed them. The building's over past my place, he wouldn't drive by it." Janet gave an exasperated exhale. "But if he's just avoiding Rob…"

"That's what I was thinking. It took Henry so long to put the war behind him. Rob could bring all that back."

Janet shook her head. "I've been seeing a lot of Rob. He let go of all that anger years ago. He doesn't talk about 'Nam or politics anymore. He's like the guy we knew in high school, but better with age, of course."

"Are you thinking you and Rob might get together?"

"No!" Janet laughed. "He's always been like a brother to me."

"Good. That will keep life simple if Henry still doesn't want to see him." Cathy resumed walking at a brisk pace.

Janet shook her head as she rushed to catch up. "They were best friends before…"

"I know, but we haven't heard from him since the wedding."

"Well, he found me on Facebook a year ago and we've been talking ever since. I tell you, he's not the way you remember. He doesn't drink, for one thing—and for crying out loud, it's been over forty years, Cath." Janet took Cathy's arm to make her stop and face her.

Cathy removed Janet's hand gently. "Maybe, but Henry hasn't had any problems since Tina was in grade school. We manage stress, keep it to a minimum… I don't want to chance messing that up. Life is good. Seeing Rob might take Henry back."

Janet remembered how hard it had been for Cathy when Tina was small and Henry's moods were still unpredictable. She put her hands up in surrender. "Okay. I'll leave it alone."

The next day, Henry drove Tina to the international airport two hours away while Cathy stayed home with the kids. Tina insisted on saying goodbye to them at the house—they couldn't wait at the gate with her and wave while the plane took off, so why subject them to all that time in the car? Henry had to agree she had a point, though he'd have enjoyed the company on the ride home.

"I can park and help you with your luggage until you check Big Blue." Henry pulled the huge suitcase out of the car. Tina had already nixed an escort all the way to security.

"Not necessary, Dad." She looped the handgrips of her computer bag over the extended handle of the suitcase so it would ride safely on top, then hitched the strap of her flight-sized purse up higher on her shoulder.

She wasn't crying, but her eyes were shiny. "Make sure the kids are ready for my call every night."

Henry pulled her into a bear hug. "We'll take good care of them, don't worry."

"I don't know what I'd do without you and Mom."

"Probably sling burgers at McDonald's," he teased.

It worked. She laughed and gently punched his arm. "I love you."

"We love you too, Honey, and the kids. You make life worth living." He gently touched her cheek.

She gave him one last hug. "See you the end of August."

He nodded, then watched her turn and head inside, pulling her luggage with her back straight. Her pace picked up after she went through the doors. He felt a surge of pride. They'd raised an independent, strong woman—and smart. When she decided to stay home with the kids, she kept up her business contacts, so when the idiot took off to find himself and left her with more debts than income, she landed a good job right away.

Henry knew she'd be fine. However, in case her flight was canceled or something, he drove to a nursery near the airport to window shop until she was in the air. They'd already planted the garden; there wasn't really anything he needed. They definitely had enough trees. The old apple orchard was one of the reasons they bought their mini-farm back when Tina was a baby. He'd spent weekends and vacation days clearing brush and pruning the trees until they had a decent crop every year. And they'd put in semi-dwarf peaches and cherries closer to the house. Still, he wandered through the fruit trees at the store.

Then he saw the tag: Cortland Apple. Cathy swore Cortlands were the best pie apple. He'd always meant to surprise her with one, but with the orchard it had seemed silly. *Better late than never.*

He decided on a dwarf tree that was already approaching his height. They might get a few apples off it this season – they'd definitely have enough for a pie in a year or two. He flagged down a store employee. "Can you take that tree up front for me?"

"Certainly."

Henry called Tina to tell her.

"Great, Dad. She'll love that... I'm already on board and I was about to put my phone on airplane mode."

"Okay. Love you."

"Love you too."

Waiting to pay for the tree, Henry glanced out the display window, and his core froze in recognition as he met the gaze of a large bald man staring at him from the sidewalk.

"Is that all, sir?"

Henry's attention swiveled to the clerk and he nodded, then he looked back out the window. The man was gone. *I imagined it. Even if there was someone out there, they weren't staring at me, and it wasn't him.*

Henry barely remembered the drive home. He spent the afternoon planting Cathy's Cortland Apple, but digging the hole didn't just leave his muscles sore, it gave his thoughts time to wander places he didn't want them to go—shadows of memories better left behind.

That night Henry woke up with his heart pounding, sweat pouring off him, his throat tight. He looked over at Cathy. She seemed to be sleeping peacefully. He was glad he hadn't disturbed her. *It couldn't have been him.*

Sunday, July 3, 2022

Henry spent Sunday morning polishing his beloved '49 Mercury convertible while Cathy took the kids to church. He'd bought the car when he got back from 'Nam. For years, it had only come out for parades and other special occasions. Now he drove it all the time, but he wanted it to really shine for the Fourth of July parade.

He finished just as Cathy and the kids got home—and rain started hitting the metal roof above him. *Good thing I parked in the barn.*

Nice big thunderstorms rolled through the rest of the day, so the four of them played Monopoly for hours. When Tommy finally won, Annie demanded they play Clue. She always chose Miss Scarlet for her token. They handed Henry Colonel Mustard, his usual character, though today he'd rather have used the purple piece than one associated with the military, however slim the connection. The game was all about solving the murder before anyone else.

Henry wrestled with another mystery while they played. How could a glimpse of that man at the nursery leave him so unsettled? He kept replaying that moment. He bounced between assuring himself that some slight similarity was all it had been, a trick of the light—and the chilling certainty that his fears were well-based.

Then he'd remind himself he'd been in the city, nowhere near home. *He wouldn't come back here, even if it was him.*

"Grandpa, it's your move," Tommy complained. "You're not paying attention."

"You're just afraid you'll lose," Annie snarked at her little brother. "Grandpa's probably figuring it all out in his head to make an accusation."

"No, Annie, my mind was wandering," Henry admitted. He saw the worried look on Cathy's face and lied. "Thinking about where we might camp this summer."

"You're really quitting your job for us?" Annie looked skeptical.

"That's the plan." Henry grinned. He could feel Cathy's continued concern despite his cheerful tone. *She can tell it's forced. She knows me too well... But she doesn't really know me at all.*

Monday, July 4, 2022

On Monday, Cathy waved at spectators on her side of the Mercury as it moved slowly along with the parade. Then she looked past Henry to wave at people on that side of the street. Her stomach tensed when he gave his head a violent shake, then relaxed when he seemed to go back to normal.

He probably thinks he hasn't woken me up with his nightmares.

She'd learned years ago to play possum. Letting him know he'd disturbed her only increased his agitation.

He seems to be enjoying the day.

Henry loved holidays like this, showing off his beloved Mercury. At the end of the parade, they followed the other classic cars to the VIP parking area—a field where they'd be safe from scratches, dings, and casually thrown fireworks.

"I'll stay with the car until people stop coming to admire them," he said.

That's normal. Cathy nodded. "We've got this." She slung the strap of the picnic blanket over Tommy's thin shoulder, handed Annie a camp chair in its bag, then hiked the strap of the other chair over her own shoulder as she grabbed a large bag of waters.

"We've got a blanket, what do we need the chairs for?" Tommy demanded.

"I can still sit on a blanket, but getting up is a spectacle." Cathy chuckled.

"Huh?"

"They're old." Annie exhaled, exasperated with her little brother. "They've got arthritis and that makes them stiff."

"Arthuritis?"

The old couple exchanged a smile.

Cathy said, "We'll check out the craft booths on our way to the lake."

Tommy whined. "Aren't we going to go on the rides?"

"I'll take you on them and do some of the games with you later." Henry grinned at Cathy. "Carnivals are not your grandmother's idea of a good time. Your mom and I always went without her. Cath, leave me some water. Be less weight."

"I should have thought of that." She handed him two of the re-purposed juice bottles she had filled at home that morning—their spring water tasted better than the town fountains. "Stay hydrated." She blew him a kiss. "Let's go kids."

They were halfway across the field when a snapper went off behind them. Someone shouted at the culprit for bringing it into the classic car area. The kids didn't notice, but Cathy turned. Henry was facing away from them, breathing the way the therapist taught him—slow deep breaths, hands pressing against his thighs.

They'd never stayed for fireworks when Tina was little. Instead, they'd always walked up the hill, where the noise was distant and the bursts of light weren't on top of them. Still, it was torture for Henry. He'd flinch with each whistle and boom. When Tina was nine, she patted his hand and said they could go home, she didn't have to watch the pretty fireworks if it scared him. He'd realized then that his problems were not his alone, and he finally agreed to get help.

With counseling, he'd gotten better. By the time Tina hit her teens, they'd been able to watch fireworks in the park with everyone else, loud and bright. The nightmares stopped as he became focused on the present and looked forward to the future.

Maybe he's seen Rob in town. Maybe that's what's bothering him.

"Come on, Grandma." Tommy had come back to pull on Cathy's hand.

Henry was tilting his head side to side, stretching his neck. That meant the episode was over; he was relaxing again. Cathy spun around and resumed walking with the kids before Henry could catch her watching.

"I don't know how much you'll like the craft booths," she said.

But Annie found a pair of earrings she positively adored. Tommy flitted ahead while Cathy completed the purchase.

"Can you see him?" Cathy asked Annie while she counted her change.

"No."

The two of them hurried along, barely glancing at the booths. Then Cathy saw Rob talking to a customer in the midst of his photographs. She paused, he glanced up, and for a moment their eyes met. The immediate sense of connection startled her.

Then Tommy re-appeared and dragged them on to a booth all about dragons—dragon posters, dragon miniatures, dragon T-shirts. Cathy let him choose a shirt.

By the time they got to the lake, Janet had joined them. The two women spread out the blanket and Annie helped set up the chairs. Other people were already staking out their spots the same way.

Cathy pulled cash out of her pocket and handed it to her granddaughter. "You can each have some caramel corn *or* cotton candy, not both. Then come straight back here."

"There's lemonade and stuff, too." Annie still had her hand out with the money.

Cathy patted her large bag. "We have water."

Annie sighed and put the cash in her pocket. "Okay. Come on, Tommy. Let's get some caramel corn."

"Cotton candy's more special."

They continued arguing as they walked away.

Cathy called after them, "Stay together!" She rolled her shoulders before sitting in one of the chairs.

Janet pulled the other chair close to her friend. "You're worried about something."

Cathy rubbed the back of her neck. "Henry was fine Friday night, wasn't he?"

"Yeah, it seemed like he enjoyed the day. He ate three helpings of my potato salad."

Cathy nodded. "He was fine until Tina left Saturday. The past two nights, he's woken me up thrashing around in his sleep, calling out for Dave the way he used to. I don't know if it's his PTSD coming back or what—or why."

"Do you want me to ask Rob to talk to him, make the first move?"

"No!" Cathy shook her head and sighed. "I was thinking maybe he saw Rob, and that's what upset him? Or maybe it's the stress of Tina flying off so far away. He took her to the airport by himself."

"That's probably it—it won't last."

"I hope so. If he gets as bad as he was before counseling... I don't know if I can go through that again. I love him, but..."

Janet reached over and put her arm around her friend. "It'll work out."

Henry had never hit Cathy on purpose, but he had bruised her thrashing out in his nightmares and several times he'd grabbed her too hard when he was startled. Cathy never let her parents know, but they had seen his mood swings. Her father had suspected.

Cathy shook off her worries. *There's been none of that for twenty years. Janet's got to be right, he'll be okay soon.*

Annie came back with caramel corn and Tommy with cotton candy.

"We decided to get one of each and share." Annie smiled proudly.

The kids had just finished their treats when Henry joined them.

"Ready to go on some rides?" He didn't need to say it twice. In a flash, the kids were up and tugging him toward the carnival. He called back over his shoulder, laughing. "See you about six!"

Once they were out of earshot, Janet turned to Cathy. "He seems okay."

"I hope so." *Annie's got common sense, if anything does go wrong.*

It was almost seven when the kids sprinted ahead of Henry, rushing to tell Cathy and Janet about the rides and games they'd played, their voices overlapping as if one.

"Grandpa says we can go back after dark and ride the Ferris wheel. But first, after we eat, we're going to watch the fireworks up on the hill like Mom did when she was a kid! Family tradition!"

Cathy was not fooled, but she was relieved Henry was taking steps to control whatever was happening with him. She smiled at the kids, "They'll burst right in front of us, instead of overhead! You'll love it."

The Bad Man

Henry got through the grand finale by focusing on all the fun he'd had with his grandchildren at the carnival, every goofy thing Tommy had said, the way Annie smoothed her hair after rides. He'd started the fireworks completely relaxed. When the last boom had popped and people below started heading for their cars, he smiled. *That wasn't so bad. I even oo'd and ah'd a couple of times with the kids.*

Tommy tugged at his hand. "Grandpa, you said you'd take us back to the Ferris wheel 'cause it's more fun at night."

Janet had watched the fireworks with them. Now she volunteered to give Cathy a ride home. "We can take the chairs and blanket with us. I'm parked up near the road."

Cathy folded her chair. "I'd love the ride home."

"Sure you don't want a romantic ride with me, on the Ferris wheel?" Henry teased.

Cathy shook her head. "You know I don't like heights. Thank you very much for the thought, though." She gave him a quick peck on the cheek.

He gave her a half-smile and a wink that said he was looking forward to more later.

Her eyes sparkled in return, then she turned to the kids, all business. "Stay close to your grandfather. No running off ahead in the dark."

"Yes, ma'am," two voices replied in chorus.

They hurried to the Ferris wheel with their grandfather. There was a long wait, but as Henry had expected, they loved riding it at night. It was more mystical.

"Can we go again?" Annie pleaded as the wheel slowly lowered them to earth.

"Sure," said Henry.

But the line was at least twice as long when the ride ended—it was mostly couples holding hands—and the fellow running the ride was counting back while the wheel began to move with a new group of riders. He stopped and put his arm between two couples. "If you're not in front of me, you're not getting onto the last ride."

The kids moaned.

"At least we got one ride at night," said Annie.

"Can we get a funnel cake?" Tommy begged. "We didn't have one before."

"It's awfully late." But Henry let himself be pulled to the line for funnel cakes. "We'll do one game on our way out."

"The darts? Where they have that big panda?" Annie perked right up when her grandfather agreed, then tried to pretend she wasn't excited about a stuffed animal.

As they waited for their turn to order funnel cakes, booths and rides began shutting down.

"They're going to close the darts," Annie fretted. "Can I go ahead?"

"I promised your grandmother we'd stay together."

"Please? I don't really care about funnel cake. The darts are right behind the ring toss." She pointed. "I can wait there for you."

They were next in line. It would only be a few minutes. Henry gave Annie money for tickets and let her go while he stayed with Tommy. He was nervous when she turned out of sight, but Tommy was already telling the vendor he wanted powdered sugar on his funnel cake.

Annie was hugging the panda bear when they caught up to her. The booth was closing.

"You won it that fast? It's as big as me!" Tommy reached out to it.

Annie turned her back to him. "Don't touch it with your greasy, sugary hands."

Henry chuckled. "Tear off a piece for your sister, then finish that up, Tommy. You can't have it in the car."

Tommy dutifully tore off a small piece for his sister and another for his grandpa.

"Just put it in my mouth," said Annie. "I don't want to get my new bear sticky."

Tommy devoured the rest as they ambled along.

Annie hugged her panda like a big baby. "Everyone's going the other way."

"The regular parking's up by the front entrance. We're probably the last car left out in the VIP lot," Henry explained.

"It's dark this way."

"It's not far." Henry pulled out his cell phone and turned on the flashlight. "Tommy, are you done with that?"

"Yup!" Tommy ran back to a trash can to toss out the paper.

Henry and Annie turned around to watch Tommy. Suddenly, someone slammed into Henry's shoulder from behind, giving him a jolt. Henry turned to say something angry like "Watch where you're going!" but the flashlight illuminated the man's face. His eyes were dark pits locking onto Henry's terrified gaze. The man didn't speak; he just lifted the corners of his mouth so his teeth showed. Henry's insides turned to ice.

The man passed by and disappeared toward the mostly-darkened carnival.

Blood pounded in Henry's ears and he stopped breathing. *He saw the kids with me. What if he saw them earlier? I let Annie go ahead of us.*

Tommy ran to Annie and grabbed her hand.

"What's wrong?" Annie asked her little brother.

"That man looked like a shark when he smiled."

Annie rolled her eyes. "Don't be silly."

"You didn't see his face."

"Whatever." Annie peered toward the carnival, but all she saw was the man's back as he passed under a light near the dart booth. It could have been the stranger who gave her the panda, but that man didn't look like a shark. He'd been nice. He might have been bald, but he was wearing a hat then. She decided she'd better keep letting Grandpa and Tommy think she'd won the prize herself.

Henry started breathing as the man disappeared. "Let's go."

He grabbed his grandchildren's hands, heedless of stickiness, and set a brisk pace back to the car. He rushed them as they rinsed their hands. "That's good enough."

"What about yours, Grandpa?" Annie took the water bottle and poured the end over Henry's hands.

He shook them off, grabbed the empty bottle and tossed it into the trunk with the towel. "Get in the car," he ordered. He slammed the trunk shut.

At home, he told the kids to brush their teeth and get into their pajamas. "We'll check on you in a minute."

Cathy was in bed, wearing the negligee she saved for special nights.

Henry remembered their parting banter and was relieved she'd fallen asleep. *No way could I make love to her now.*

He went to tuck in each of the kids. Annie was a quick goodnight.

Tommy wanted to talk. "That shark man, Grandpa. Who was he?"

Henry weighed reassuring his grandson with protecting him. "You're right, Tommy, he is a bad man, and if you ever see him again, tell me right away. But you probably won't. He was just playing a mean joke on me."

"Okay." The exhausted little boy accepted the explanation and yawned.

"And Tommy, probably don't talk about him with Annie or your Grandma. There's no reason to worry the girls when we probably won't ever see him again."

Tommy fell asleep mid-nod.

Henry didn't have nightmares that night. He didn't sleep at all.

Blackmail

Tuesday, July 5, 2022

The first call came the next day, on the landline in Henry's office.

He didn't have a secretary; he actually could have continued working from home after the pandemic. But it was a small town. Sometimes clients liked to drop by to talk. The building he was in housed an antique store on the street side, and his office on the back. Upstairs, a dentist had the front rooms and Steve Hillman had his office in the back. A corridor with stairs and separate entrances for each place of business ran from the Main Street sidewalk to the employee parking behind the building.

The insurance company's number was listed in the slim phone book's yellow pages, along with Henry's name and photo.

The voice on the phone made the hairs on the back of Henry's neck stick up—so familiar, yet so different. Henry tried asking questions, tried starting a conversation, but all he got back was a short demand. He felt sweat trickle from his armpits down his sides as he listened. Five thousand dollars, used cash, nothing bigger than a twenty.

"I can do it this once, but we don't have much. I mean, look at me, man, I'm seventy years old and still working." Henry's plea was met with silence. "I can get it this afternoon. Do you want to meet me at the bank? It's over in Winton."

Instead, he was given instructions to put the twenties into a supermarket bag and leave it at the corner of Old Mill and Cemetery Road.

Henry debated telling Cathy, but he hoped this would be the end of it. After all, there hadn't been any contact since that night so long ago. *Maybe he's down on his luck, maybe it will just be this once. He only asked for money. He didn't make any threats.*

But Henry didn't really believe that. Tommy was right. Those were shark's eyes, devoid of feeling. So he picked up the money and put it into a plastic grocery bag.

When he got to the drop-off corner, in the middle of nowhere, he pulled over and waited in the car. It was a beautiful day. He had the top down on the Merc.

He really wants me to leave that much money here? In a grocery bag?

The corner was clear for a good ten yards in any direction, but then there were trees, lots of trees with dense undergrowth.

He could be parked on a logging road, watching me. I'd never know if—no. He wants money. He wouldn't take me out.

Henry wasn't sure he believed this.

A lone car with two teenagers came from the opposite direction and paused beside him. The driver rolled down his window. "Everything okay Mister? You need help?"

"Pulled over for a call." Henry held up his cell phone. "Thanks anyway."

When they had disappeared around a curve, he finally got out of the car with the bag. He looked around, found a decent-sized rock to weigh it down, and put the bag about ten feet into the field from the stop sign.

That's too obvious.

He took the rock off the bag, put it inside instead and tied the handles together. The plastic moved slightly in the breeze.

That looks better, like someone tossed trash out their window.

He got back into his car and sat a few moments, not sure whether he was hoping for a conversation or just reluctant to leave that kind of money sitting in the open like that. Finally, he turned the key and drove away.

Hopefully that's the end of it.

***

Once Henry was gone, an old pickup drove out of the woods. The man from the fair picked up the bag and removed the rock. He grinned at the cash.

That was easy. This is going to be fun.

Wednesday, July 6, 2022

Henry woke up to the smell of coffee. Still on his side with knees pulled to his chest, he remembered the images that had plagued him in his sleep.

He won't stop. He wants to ruin my life.

Henry forced himself to stretch out on his back and tried to convince himself he was wrong. He practiced his deep breathing until he accepted he'd have to wait and see what the day brought. He got up, dressed quickly, and headed downstairs.

He knew Cathy was worried. She couldn't help but know he was having nightmares again. But now she was bustling around the kitchen as cheerful as he'd seen her since Tina left. *Was that really only four days ago?*

Cathy was washing strawberries she'd just brought in from the garden and had his favorite sour cream coffeecake in the oven. Combined with the coffee she'd already made, the aroma was heavenly. Her half-empty mug sat on the counter near her. It almost felt like a normal day.

Henry inhaled deeply. "That should get those sleepy-head kids out of bed." He grabbed his favorite mug and filled it from the glass pot. "Can I help?"

"I've got it. Sit, enjoy your coffee. I'll be done with this in a minute."

Once she finished washing berries, Cathy left them to drain. She topped up her coffee and sat at the table with her husband. Her whole being smiled. "I am so happy you're retiring. What did they say? When is your last day?"

Henry's face fell. He'd forgotten that promise. There was no way he could retire now, not until he was sure the blackmail was done.

Five thousand's probably not the end of it.

He looked at his coffee instead of Cathy's face. "Um... I didn't give notice yet."

"What?" The word burst out of her. Then her voice turned cold, like it had when Tina was little and she was done with his claims he didn't need help. "Why not?"

He couldn't blame her for being furious. *And I promised the kids we'd do that big tour of National Parks. Everyone's going to be mad at me.* He'd retire immediately if he thought the blackmail would stop. But he didn't. "I'm not sure we can afford it yet."

"Friday you were sure we could." She got up, too agitated to sit. "Well, if you're not going to retire, I may take the kids on a National Parks tour by myself."

Henry's chest tightened, thinking of that grin—a shark's smile, like Tommy said. The threat didn't have to be voiced. Henry wasn't sure if Cathy and their grandchildren would be safer away by themselves or staying close to home. He knew he'd worry about them more if they were far away camping.

"We should watch expenses until things get straightened out." At least this was not a lie. He managed to face her.

Cathy blew an air raspberry. "Camping's not that expensive. I already have my Senior Pass for the Parks, and we'll be cooking food the same as if we were home. It'll only be gas."

"The pass gets you into the parks, but it doesn't cover campsites, and camping rates have gone up a lot since we used to take Tina."

Cathy crossed her arms. "Then you tell them. You got them so excited about it. They spent all day yesterday researching parks, deciding where we should go, what we should do. If you hadn't gotten home so late last night, you'd know that."

"I had to work." This was true, too—he'd had paperwork to finish that got put aside while he got the blackmail money and delivered it per instructions.

"Well, *you* be the one to tell them. As if they haven't had enough heartache."

Annie and Tommy came into the kitchen sniffing the air.

The timer for the coffeecake went off. Cathy gave Henry a glare, then went to get it out of the oven.

There was a lead weight in Henry's stomach. *Get this over with.*

"I've got some bad news, kids. I can't retire as soon as I planned."

"So, like a couple more weeks?" Tommy's eyebrows shoveled together.

Henry shook his head. "I'm not sure, Tommy. It could be longer."

"What he means is we won't be going on any big trip. Forget National Parks." Annie whipped around and stomped back to her room.

Tommy crumpled. "Like when Dad said we'd do stuff."

The disappointment on his grandson's face wrenched Henry's heart. But there was nothing he could say to make it better. He watched Tommy shuffle out of the kitchen.

Cathy had the coffeecake on a trivet and now stood at the sink, putting strawberries in a bowl, her back to him.

He tried to bring the day back to normal. *She won't be as angry later.* "Save me a piece of that coffeecake."

She didn't offer to send a piece with him. She didn't respond or look at him at all.

Shortly after Henry got to work, the phone rang with another demand for five thousand.

I need to write a letter for Cathy, in case something happens to me, so she can understand. He spent the rest of the morning writing and revising and re-writing the letter. Explaining on paper was cathartic. He decided to write two more and put them into addressed, stamped envelopes. He put those in the bottom drawer of his desk with a sticky note: Personal. Mail if anything happens to me. *Someone will find them if I'm gone.*

He put Cathy's letter into an envelope with her name on it. He took it with him when he drove to Winton to get the blackmailer's cash. Henry had a few insurance clients there, so no one would question the trips. However, when he handed the teller a withdrawal slip for five thousand dollars and again asked for it in twenties, she balked.

"I'm sorry, sir, but I'm going to have to ask you to process this withdrawal with our manager, Mrs. Roberts."

Mrs. Roberts came to escort him to her cubicle. "Please come with me. You have your identification with you?"

"There's enough in the account," he protested, but he pulled out his wallet as he followed her.

Once she verified his identity, she apologized. "Aside from small deposits twice a year, just enough to keep it open, there's been no activity on this account since it was opened more than forty years ago,. Then there was a withdrawal Tuesday, and now another. Well, you understand our caution."

"Certainly." In fact, their caution was a good thing.

"We can do a direct transfer. That would be safer. Or a bank check."

"No, I prefer cash."

"Are you sure you don't want larger bills? It would be less bulky."

"I came prepared." He pulled the plastic grocery bag out of his pocket.

He didn't bother to request used bills. That would really disturb her. He could always provide wear and tear on any new ones. "While I'm here, I'd like to check the safety deposit box, too. And can you make sure my wife still has access to that?"

Cathy had signed for the box the first week they were married, but then they opened their joint account and she probably assumed he'd closed this one. He'd certainly never given her a key to the safety deposit box.

"Her signature is here, but her name's not on the bank account. That's unusual." Mrs. Roberts' pursed lips expressed her distaste for yet another deviation from normal.

"It was mine before we got married. I added her name to the box in case anything happened to me, so she'd be able to get my will and all."

"Oh, well, I guess that's acceptable." She looked through the record. "She's never accessed it."

"I'll have to make sure our lawyer knows about it. My wife's probably forgotten it exists." That's what he had intended.

Henry took the safety deposit box into a private room. He had to be sure everything was still there in the manila envelope and reluctantly went through it. Most of the contents he loathed touching, but he put one photo in his pocket. He closed the manila envelope and left the letter for Cathy separate, on top. As long as she read the letter first, she wouldn't have to see the rest. The photo was for one of the other letters.

Hopefully she'll never need to know about that.

***

The man inside the old pickup watched Henry leave the bank and frowned.

What took him so long?

Thursday, July 7, 2022

Henry woke up with his heart pounding. He sat up, blinking, and realized he'd fallen asleep at his desk at work.

No surprise. Five nights with little or no sleep. I'm not a kid.

He'd had to go to Winton again this morning.

That account was his combat pay, with decades of accumulated interest. It was his safety net if the market and his retirement account crashed—a last resort, money he never really wanted to use. Money Cathy didn't know about. By the time he proposed to her, he'd built up a decent amount of savings at another bank. That was what he closed when they got married and combined their banking in a joint account. He'd let Cathy assume his contribution included whatever he had in Winton.

The demand was for five thousand again, dropped off the same way.

He's toying with me.

Henry thought it through. *If money was the point, he'd ask for more and be done with it. He wants to hurt me.*

But he doesn't know I have those photos of him.

The steady temperature in the bank vault had kept them in surprisingly good condition.

But if the rest came out? I'd lose everything.

He called Cathy's cell to check on her.

"Hi. What's up?" Her voice was cheerful, unworried.

At least she's talking to me. He fumbled for something to say. "Just wanted to ask how your day is going."

"Fine..."

She was suspicious, worried about his mental health again. He could hear it in her voice.

I've got to say something normal. She said something about her sister visiting. Today? Tomorrow?

He was taking too long.

Cathy's voice was full of concern. "Are you okay? How is *your* day going?"

Not well, not well at all. "Fine."

"Suzie called. They'll be here tomorrow afternoon. The kids are excited to spend time with their cousins."

"Great—think I'll come home to work. It's nicer than the office."

Friday, July 8, 2022

Henry decided to work from home on Friday, too. He didn't want to leave Cathy and the kids alone. The nearest neighbor was a half mile away, down the road around a curve, out of sight. Normally he liked that privacy, but now it worried him.

The kids were distantly polite at breakfast, then avoided him.

They think I'm like their idiot father, making promises and never following through.

Mid-morning, Cathy came up behind him and rubbed his shoulders. "You're tense."

There was no point in denying it, but he wasn't about to explain. "I have a lot of calls to make." Calls—he always calls on the office landline. *What if he can't reach me?* "Is our landline still listed?"

Cathy kept massaging his shoulders. "Yes, and we're on a private line if you want to use it for work. Remember what it was like sharing the line with Johnsons?"

Henry nodded. "She is such a gossip."

"I don't know how you're so nice to her." Cathy felt the muscles under her fingers softening.

"What was I supposed to do, drive right past her when she kept getting stuck in her own driveway?" *We're having a normal conversation. This is good. Maybe she's forgiving me.*

"I think she was trying to get you to plow for her."

"No. Her husband has a lawn tractor with a blade. I've seen him use it... How soon is Suzie getting here?"

"By lunchtime."

"I should go to the office before they arrive. It'll be quieter to work."

Before he left, he unplugged the landline—the phone downstairs and the one in their bedroom, by the wall, where no one would notice. He didn't want the blackmailer talking to Cathy or one of the kids.

They always use their cell phones, anyway.

At the office, Henry used the phone as little as possible, to leave the line open for his blackmailer, but no call came.

Five o'clock.

Henry clicked his pen over and over, unsure whether or not he should leave.

What if he tried this morning while I was still at home? What if he's going after Cathy and the kids now? He doesn't just want money.

But Henry had checked in with Cathy shortly after noon. Suzie and her grandkids were there.

Two adults, two teenage boys, Annie, and Tommy. Safety in numbers. Maybe.

Henry looked at the mess on his desk. He wasn't getting anything done.

Go home. He'll know not to call me here on the weekend. As long as he didn't try this morning.

Halfway up the driveway, Henry spotted the tent in the yard, the one they'd always used when Tina was growing up.

No! They can't be out here tonight. His knuckles turned white as he clenched the steering wheel.

He wants to ruin my life. Payback for ruining his. He probably called today. I should have been at the office this morning. Now he's mad.

Henry parked and got out of the car, staring at the tent.

Tommy came rushing up and started pulling at Henry's hand. "Look, Grandpa. We're going to camp right here in the yard!"

"No. It's not safe."

Tommy stared at Henry in disbelief, then burst into tears and ran inside the house.

Henry stomped over to the tent, where Annie and her two cousins were putting in the last pegs. "You can play out here tomorrow, but it's not safe to sleep outside."

"What?" Annie stared at him in disbelief.

"I've heard coyotes at night, and people say there may be a cougar around."

Cathy and Suzie had come up behind him, towed by Tommy.

"Are you serious?" Suzie glared at him. "That's ridiculous. They'll be inside the tent. And there haven't ever been any cougars in this area."

Henry crossed his arms. "I've heard the coyotes myself. They'll attack a kid Tommy's size."

Cathy had her arm around Tommy. "Henry, there've never been coyotes in this yard. And like Suzie said, the kids will be in the tent."

"That's nothing but a flimsy nylon wall." Henry shook his head.

"You weren't worried when that buffalo brushed up against it on his way through the campground at Yellowstone! *You* calmed *me* down." Cathy stomped off to the house, Suzie right behind her.

The teenagers tried to reason with him to no avail.

Annie grimaced in disgust. She scanned her grandfather head to toe and back. "You're worse than my father." She headed for the house. "Come on, Tommy."

The cousins followed, leaving Henry alone in the yard.

Annie hates me.

Henry watered the new apple tree, then walked the perimeter of their property. When he finally got back to the house, the kids were all in the tent playing cards by flashlight. He paused outside the kitchen door. Cathy and Suzie were talking while they cleaned up after the dinner they'd eaten without him.

"He's nuts, Cathy. I don't know why you didn't divorce him when Tina was a baby. You may have fooled the folks, but I saw fingerprints on your arms. I know you said he went to counseling and yes, it seemed to be better all these years, but not anymore. He's nuts. You need to walk away."

Cathy didn't answer, didn't defend him.

If she finds out why this is happening, she'll leave me for sure.

Henry grabbed a cup of coffee and a banana while Cathy ignored him. Everyone else was still sleeping. His heart squeezed at the possibility of losing her.

It's my seventy-first birthday today. Do you remember? Do the kids even know it's my birthday? "I'm going into the office. I'm behind on paperwork and you'll enjoy your visit with Suzie more without me." *Please, say something.*

Cathy nodded and turned away to put something into the sink.

Just don't let her convince you to divorce me.

He managed to focus on his paperwork and reach the clients who were easier to contact on a Saturday. By late afternoon, he was caught up. The office phone rang when he was about to head home. He answered it without thinking.

"Henry Clark. How can I help you?"

"Happy birthday, Henry. Did you think I was done with you?"

Henry's heart skipped a beat, then raced. "Tell me how much you want. However much it'll take for you to leave us alone."

"They wouldn't give you that much in cash, and I don't take checks. Besides, I'm having fun tormenting you, Henry. You'll never know when I'm going to call." A short demented chuckle came through the phone. Then, "It's fun to know *you* are terrified of *me*. What took you so long at the bank the other day?"

Henry took a deep breath. *I have to chance it.* "I was checking on my photo collection. Photos of you. At work."

"I don't have anything, any*one* to lose, Henry. You do."

"You wouldn't hurt Cathy."

"Does she know what you did?" There was a long silence before the man continued. "I didn't think so."

Dial tone.

Henry stared at the receiver as he slowly replaced it on the phone base. His entire body started shaking.

Cathy will leave me if she ever finds out. He won't hurt her, but he'll tell her. Whatever happened to him, wherever he's been, it's my fault. It's because of what I did. But if I'm wrong...

If Cathy was in physical danger, he had to do whatever he could to protect her. *At night, when I'm sleeping, he could walk right in and...* Henry got to the hardware store just before they closed.

***

"There's no way I am staying to celebrate his birthday." Suzie handed a brightly wrapped package to Cathy. "It's an apron for when he barbeques. Tell him I didn't feel well, that I wanted to get home and be wretched in my own bed."

Before they left, Cathy had the teenage boys help pack up the tent.

"Why can't we keep sleeping in it?" complained Tommy. "It was nice."

Annie just threw Cathy a sullen look. When Cathy set out art materials for them to make birthday cards for their grandpa, Annie put in minimal effort. Tommy at least enjoyed drawing a picture of a tent and campfire on his.

Cathy made the sloppy joes Henry liked, some macaroni salad, and grape pie, his favorite birthday dessert. *I should at least have invited Janet. He'd rather have her potato salad.*

Cathy was too angry with him to celebrate. *Good thing I bought his present a month ago.*

She'd seen a book he didn't have, one on vintage cars that included a photo of a Mercury convertible just like his baby. Tina had left behind a wrapped car cleaning kit from her and the kids.

Henry got home at dinnertime and they all wished him a happy birthday. They had a pleasant enough dinner, sang the birthday song as he blew out a seven and a one candle on his grape pie, then accepted his thanks when he opened presents. The kids helped clean the kitchen quickly and went to set up Michigan Rummy on the dining room table.

Cathy was drying the iron skillet when Henry came into the kitchen and put a new deadbolt on the back door. She held back her questions until after they played cards and the kids were in bed. Then he started shutting and latching all the windows as well as the new deadbolts on the front and back doors.

"We need to let the cool night air in or the house will be hot as Hades by midday." Cathy tried to keep a pleasant tone.

"It's not safe."

"You'll be at work, the heat won't bother you." She started unlatching windows to let in the night breeze. "Go ahead and bolt the doors, but the windows need to be open."

He went behind her re-latching them. "Anyone could get in here through one of these windows. We can leave the ones upstairs open. I put a chain lock on the tall ladders so no one can use them to get in."

She stopped to stare at him and shake her head, then went back to unlocking windows.

He stopped following her around. "I'm going to lock them before I go to bed."

"Hope you're planning on staying up late." Cathy finished opening windows, then went into the kitchen to get a glass of water. When she came back, Henry was sitting, slumped over the dining room table, staring down blankly.

Cathy sat next to him and grabbed his hands. She waited until he met her gaze to speak. "Henry, you need to get back into counseling. Please. This is getting ridiculous and I don't know how much I can take. I'm not as patient as I was twenty years ago."

"You were patient?" He tried to make it a joke, but it fell flat. "Yeah, you were patient. Just... trust me. Please. This is different."

"The nightmares are every night, screaming for Dave. It has never been that bad. And you're being paranoid, Henry. No one shuts themselves in like this at night. Not here. Please, go back to the counselor you worked with before, or go to the VA, or come to church with us tomorrow and talk with the pastor. You liked him."

Henry looked like he could cry. "Please, trust me Cathy."

She dropped his hands, stared at him for a long moment, then shook her head and pushed back her chair. She got up and walked out of the room.

Cathy curled up on the couch reading a book until she was too tired to stay up any longer. As she started up the stairs, she heard Henry closing windows.

Cathy pulled into a parking space in the lot next to the church. She got her purse and checked that the kids still looked decent after the drive.

Janet walked up to greet them. "Morning."

Cathy nodded. "Come on, kids. Out of the car. We're going to be late."

"I don't like Sunday school," Tommy grumbled. "Haven't they ever heard of summer vacation?"

Cathy gave Janet a lopsided grin and shrug.

"Honeymoon's over, eh?" Janet offered a sympathetic smile.

"I need to get these kids downstairs." Cathy stretched her neck before turning back to her grandchildren. She was tired, not angry at them. She took comfort in the normalcy of the hectic morning.

"I'll save you a spot in the back." Janet went in ahead of them.

At the top of the stairs inside, Annie turned to her grandmother, chin high. "Grandma, last week was our first time here, so it was okay for you to take us to our classes, but I'm too old for that and I can make sure Tommy goes where he's supposed to—you don't need to be hiking up and down these stairs."

Cathy was taken aback by the last bit—she didn't have any trouble using stairs. She wasn't sure if the statement showed thoughtful concern or youthful condescension toward the elderly, whether to be proud or annoyed. In either case, Annie was right that they were old enough to go to their classrooms on their own.

Cathy shooed them on with a wave of her hand. "I'll meet you by the treats."

Tommy perked up. "They do that every week? Not just last time?"

"Every week," Cathy assured him. Maybe he wouldn't fuss so much next Sunday.

The kids headed down the stairs. Cathy went into the nave, took a program from the usher, and slipped into the back pew next to Janet.

"That was quick." Janet handed her a hymnal.

"They know where their classes are now."

Cathy straightened up on the bench. She checked the numbers posted up front, leafed through the book to the first hymn to be sung, and used her program for a marker. Then, since the service had not yet started, she checked to see who all was in church.

"More than half of the people here are old women," she whispered to Janet.

"That includes us." Janet whispered back.

Cathy elbowed her friend gently, then nodded toward the altar. "It seems like yesterday Henry and I were up there saying our vows."

"How did I never get married?"

"You always fell for jerks." Cathy leaned against her friend to soften the words.

As if conjured by their conversation, Kevin walked in with the young woman he'd been seeing since he and Janet had parted ways.

Janet nodded toward Kevin's back. "Or nice guys who didn't want to commit."

"At this stage of our lives, there's not that much to commit to. It's not like you'd be starting a family."

Janet shrugged. "He's younger than me, you know. Sixty-three. He didn't think he should have a family while he was in the military and CIA. Maybe that's what he wants now. She's young enough."

"She's young enough to be his granddaughter." Cathy reminded herself she was in church and regretted making such a catty statement. "I love having my grandkids for the summer, but I'm glad Tina's independent enough to live on her own with them when she gets back. And I can't imagine anyone our age dealing with a baby day and night."

Janet was still staring at Kevin's back. "We were so good together. I really thought..."

At that point, the organist's opening chord reverberated through the air to announce the beginning of the service.

Cathy was fine until the minister started talking. Her head slowly leaned back while his voice droned on. At the first light snore, Janet's elbow poked her side hard enough to wake her up. Startled, Cathy looked around. No one seemed to have noticed. She struggled to keep quiet as her body demanded a huge yawn to replenish her oxygen.

When the service was over, Janet guided her outside instead of following everyone downstairs for the treats. "What is going on, Cath?"

"I haven't been sleeping well."

"What's happening?"

"Let's see. The nightmares are back, every night. He reneged on his promise to retire so we could spend the summer visiting National Parks with the kids—"

"No wonder they're not happy."

Cathy nodded. "My sister and her grandkids drove down Friday to spend the weekend—we figured they could camp in the yard."

"A consolation prize."

"But when Henry got home Friday night, he went off about it not being safe, coyotes, even a cougar! He did not want them to sleep out there."

"A cougar? Here?" Janet laughed. "How'd that play out?"

"The kids slept in the tent and Henry slept on the porch—if he slept."

"Seriously?" Janet's face displayed her disbelief.

"They packed up and left yesterday morning. He knew I was furious—he went into work, even though it was his birthday."

"Shoot. I completely forgot." Janet slumped.

"I've been in no mood to throw him a party. Suzie thinks I should kick him out."

"She's divorced, isn't she?"

"Yeah. Three times. But she may have a point. We had a subdued birthday dinner and while the kids and I cleaned up the kitchen, he put deadbolts on the doors!"

"No one locks doors around here!"

"He insisted on locking all the windows, too! We went back and forth on that. I stayed up as long as I could to let the cool air into the house. He locked them as soon as I started up the stairs."

"It sounds like he needs help again."

Cathy nodded energetically. "Oh yeah. In the middle of the battle of the windows, I sat him down face to face and told him I don't know how much I can take. I suggested the counselor he liked before, the V.A., even coming to church with us and talking with the pastor."

"I don't think I've seen Henry in church since your wedding. Does he even know this pastor?"

"They met at the Memorial Day parade one year and have chatted a few times since then. But Henry just kept saying this isn't the same as before and begging me to trust him." Cathy sighed and blinked to keep back tears. "It's only been a week and I'm exhausted. I don't know what to do."

Janet put her arm around her friend. "I'm going to see Rob this afternoon. Do you want me to ask him to try talking to Henry?"

"I don't know. Seeing Rob might make things worse—in fact, I was wondering if he did see Rob in town and that's what started all of this. But if it was, maybe talking to Rob is exactly what he needs." Cathy sighed again. "Let me think about it."

"Hey, how's Tina doing?"

Janet's change of topic worked. It got Cathy talking about something that was going right, so she was feeling better by the time the kids found their way outside. Tommy had cookies for both of them.

"We figured you weren't coming for the treats," said Annie. "I wasn't sure he was supposed to take them, but he wanted to do something nice."

"It's totally okay," Janet assured her. "But I'm having lunch with a friend, so I'll save mine for later.

***

Janet parked behind Rob's studio and went to the apartment entrance. She let herself in and called out as she climbed the stairs. "Hello!"

When she found no one in the apartment, she went down the interior steps to the studio. The dark room door was closed and the red light above it glowed. She knocked. "Hey, I'm here."

"Make yourself at home," Rob called through the closed door. "There's some apple juice in the refrigerator and everything's ready for lunch. I'll be done in a few minutes."

Janet decided to wander around the studio instead, looking for any additions to the scores of photographs on the walls. Some were digital, some Rob did with traditional methods. He said he liked having the option to do either.

At last he emerged from his darkroom.

"I really like this series you've got of Matt Baker at his potter's wheel."

"Thanks. I've got a few more of him and his work hanging to dry. They're part of a series I'm doing on local craftsmen. Come on upstairs. Any news on the Kevin front?"

"He's still with his sweet young thing."

"Idiot. Good for me though. Who else would look after a bachelor in his old age? Besides, you know I've always loved you." Rob threw her a grin.

"Right." She punched him gently on the arm. "We both know better than that."

Once upstairs, the conversation veered away to food preparation and casual chat. While they cleaned up, he asked why she'd been late.

"You were in the darkroom when I got here."

"Yeah, I decided to keep busy when you were ten minutes late."

"Fair enough. Cathy needed to talk."

"Is she okay?"

The urgency in Rob's voice was no surprise to Janet. She tsked and shook her head. "Are you ready to admit you've been avoiding them because of your feelings for Cathy, not because of your tiff with Henry?"

"Is she okay?" His handsome features had slid into a mask of concern.

"She's worried about him. The nightmares he used to have about Dave are back and his behavior's getting bizarre."

"Bizarre how? He hasn't hurt her, has he?"

Janet looked at the tension in Rob's body.

I never should have told him how bad it got before Henry went to counseling.

She folded her arms and stared into his eyes.

Finally he caved and said, "Fine. You're right. I still have feelings for Cathy."

Janet put a hand on Rob's forearm. "He hasn't hurt her, but he's gotten really weird and she's not sure how much more she can take, especially with their grandkids there for the summer. I was thinking maybe you could talk to him."

Rob stepped back. "You're nuts. Even if Cathy wasn't in the middle, I'm the last person he'd talk with about personal stuff, especially anything to do with Vietnam."

"Will you think about it? For Cathy?"

Rob narrowed his eyes to glare at Janet. She held his gaze until he heaved a sigh and shrugged.

Janet took that as a yes, he'd think about it.

Thursday, July 14, 2022

Henry was feeling good. It was Thursday and there hadn't been any demands or phone calls this week. *It wasn't about money, it was about payback. He got to see me scared, that's what he wanted. He's probably long gone, bored of playing with me.*

Henry opened the bottom left drawer of his desk and looked at the two stamped envelopes topped with his sticky note. *I'm glad I didn't mail those.*

Then the call came. "Five thousand. Same as before."

Henry tried being firm. "Enough with the games. Tell me how much you want and I'll get it all at once. It might take a few days to turn it into cash, but I'll do it."

A dial tone was his answer.

Henry closed the drawer. This time he got the cash out of his joint savings account with Cathy, from the bank in town.

I can replace it later. I'm going to tell her everything.

He drove out to the same field and left a note in the bag:

No more. I'm going to tell Cathy everything. I hope she won't leave me. If she does, it will be better than letting you jerk me around like this.

Henry took one last look at the bag, then the distant woods, and felt good. *That's an end to it.*

But by the time he pulled into the office parking lot, he was second-guessing himself. *I shouldn't have written that note. He's right. I have more to lose than he does. I shouldn't have told him I'll tell Cathy. He might consider her a threat. And the kids... he saw me with the kids...*

It was too late to go back and remove the note. Henry turned off the car and sat staring at the second floor window, the office of his lawyer and financial advisor, Steve Hillman.

He nodded his head, got out of the car, and chirped the lock. On the way up the interior stairs, Henry rehearsed what he was going to say. He didn't want to explain any more than necessary, but Steve was probably the only one who could help.

The front desk was empty and the door to Steve's office was open. He was at his desk, alone, intent on the papers in his hand. Henry walked in and closed the door.

Steve looked up, startled. "Janet put you down for next week. I'm really busy today."

Henry crossed to the desk and stood facing Dave Hillman's little brother. "You have to make Dave stop playing this game with me, demanding a few thousand at a time. Find out how much will make him stop."

Steve stared at Henry, speechless. His shock was clearly genuine. He blinked and shook his head. Finally he found his voice. "Dave? My brother Dave?"

He didn't know Dave's alive. Henry nodded slowly. "I told your mother. He went AWOL, I covered for him But I didn't tell her that I saw him just before I came home for good. He was working with drug runners and wasn't the Dave we knew anymore."

"He's blackmailing you? But he'd be in more trouble than you."

Henry's stomach clenched. Steve was right, except for the part only Dave knew—why he went AWOL. "Probably. But he's crazy, Steve. The way he looked at me when I was with my grandkids? I just want him to leave."

Steve sat, stunned. "I haven't heard from him. I thought he was dead."

"Maybe your mother has. Please, find out how much it'll take to make him stop."

"Of course, if I can."

Henry walked down the stairs to his own office. *Please, let money be enough.* He paced back and forth, gripping his head. *Steve really didn't know Dave's alive. Maybe I should talk to Rob. He wasn't there with us, but he must have seen enough to understand.*

***

After Henry left, Steve Hillman sat staring at his hands, then at his degrees and license to practice law, framed and proudly displayed on his office wall. *This could ruin me. I need to talk to Mother. She must know he's here.*

Friday, July 15, 2022

The next morning, Henry woke up determined to be done with fear. *Cathy loves me. She knows who I am now. That's what's important. I won't tell her anything, but if Dave does, she'll still love me. She'll understand.*

He stretched gently so he wouldn't wake his wife.

I'll work with that banker to get cash for everything I have in the Winton account. Dave may claim money's not enough, but he doesn't know how much is there.

The birds chirping outside seemed to support his positive view. *I wasn't going to use that money, ever, so I can go ahead and retire. We can take that road trip with the kids.*

Cathy was still asleep.

I won't tell her until I've got everything set up.

He slid out of bed carefully and dressed quietly. In the kitchen, he swigged down some orange juice. Needing physical activity moving in the right direction, he did a pre-trip check on all the car fluids before leaving for work—and realized the brakes needed attention immediately. He drove straight to Tony's shop, the only mechanic in town.

"You want a rush brake job? I'm booked solid today and all next week."

Henry grimaced. "I suppose I could top off the fluid, but the little that's left in the reservoir is filthy."

"Pop the hood." Tony walked over to look at Henry's engine. When he opened the brake fluid reservoir, he shook his head. "It's a miracle you haven't had the line clog up. Leave it, I'll drain it, flush it, and put in new fluid between my other jobs."

"Thanks, Tony. I owe you."

"You bet you do."

Henry walked to his office. He had paperwork to finish up on those new accounts.

I'll get everything in order here, figure out how to get cash for the Winton money, then I'll turn in my retirement papers Monday. I won't tell Cathy until it's all a done deal.

If he ever explained everything about Dave and 'Nam, it would be after Tina came back and took the kids home. That way, if Cathy wanted nothing more to do with him, at least he'd have a great summer to remember.

The hours passed without a call demanding more money or delivering a threat. The silence left Henry bouncing between his optimistic planning and then worrying about repercussions from the note and talking to Steve.

He's not really Dave anymore; I knew that when I went back and found him. What if I've pissed him off? Will he go after Cathy and the kids?

At two, he walked to Tony's garage and picked up the car. The brakes worked fine at the one stop sign on his way to the office parking lot. He backed into a space with the passenger side toward the building.

The next hour passed without another dreaded call, but instead of being relieved, Henry's fears started to outweigh his hope. He had work he should be doing, things that needed to be tidied up before he retired, but he couldn't concentrate.

The fear crept up on him.

I shouldn't have written the note. He wanted me afraid. I didn't sound afraid in the note. I said I was going to tell Cathy.

When Henry realized he was having trouble breathing, he chastised himself for being paranoid. For peace of mind, he called Cathy's cell. He got up and paced the room while it rang.

"Hi. What's up?" Her voice was pleasant, unworried.

He fumbled for something to say. "Just wanted to ask how your day is going."

"Fine. The kids helped weed the strawberries and we're going down to the creek in a little bit. How is your day going?"

Not well, not well at all. I'm going nuts here. His right foot vibrated inside his shoe. "Fine. I'm almost done."

"Are you okay?"

She was suspicious, still worried about his mental health. He could hear it in her voice. *I've got to say something normal.* He stared out at the empty parking lot. *Normal...*

A short, ironic bark of laughter erupted from his chest.

"Henry?"

I'm worrying her more. "I'll see you soon." He put the cell phone into his pocket and crossed the office to his desk. He clenched his fists to match the tightness in his chest.

I'm not getting anything done here.

His breathing shallow, he opened his hands, then pulled his car keys out of the pocket of his khakis. He stood there, staring at the keys.

He wants me to be afraid. Terrified. I deserve that. Turnabout is fair play. I shouldn't have written that note. The only way he can hurt me now is to hurt Cathy or the kids.

He ran for the door.

The Accident

Friday July 15, 2022

Cathy and the children had just come back from playing at the creek—they were still outside—when the sheriff's car pulled up the driveway. Cathy's heart stood still. She could feel a protective guard enclose it. Tommy was excited to find out why the police were there, but she barely heard his words.

She could see the message in the h's face as he got out of the car. "Annie, take Tommy upstairs. Both of you rinse off and change into dry clothes."

Tommy started to object, but Annie herded him into the house.

Edna Johnson drove in and parked next to the sheriff's car.

The deputy's words were muffled by the pressure in Cathy's ears. Bits and pieces came through. Tree. Old car. No air bag. Broken steering column. Car being towed for exam. "There were skid marks, like he was braking, but they headed right for the tree. Was he depressed or anything?"

Cathy ignored the chill around her heart and lied. "No, not at all."

Edna was walking over from her car.

The deputy nodded toward her. "Your neighbor called it in, she's here to help. I need to get back to the scene."

I need to see him. "I should go…"

He cut her off. "No ma'am. Mrs. Johnson confirmed his identity and the coroner already took him. Wait until they release the body to the funeral home and they can fix him up some. You do not need to see him right now."

The body. Then he left and she was alone with Edna Johnson—the biggest, most judgmental gossip in town.

"I can help you tell the children, dear."

No. Not you. You'll have half the town thinking it was suicide before nightfall. Cathy struggled to be polite. "Thank you, but I really need to absorb this myself before I tell the children."

"You shouldn't be alone at a time like this, dear."

"Janet is already on her way over. She was joining us for dinner." *How did I manage to lie so smoothly?*

"Well, I'll stay until she gets here." Edna took a step toward the house.

Cathy grabbed her arm. "Do you mind waiting out here? So you can explain everything to Janet? Where the children won't hear?"

"Certainly."

"I need to put on dry clothes. We were at the creek." Cathy caught a sob, turned and walked into the house.

She went first to the kitchen where her cell phone was sitting on the counter, as usual, and made a quick call to Janet. It went to voice mail. "Henry's dead. Please come as quick as you can and get rid of Edna Johnson." She sent a text saying the same and headed upstairs rehearsing how to tell the children.

Both of them were in Annie's room at the front of the house, sitting on the bed with Annie's arm around her little brother. They were crying quietly.

Annie spoke through her tears. "I heard what the policeman said, Grandma. I told Tommy myself. We'll wait up here until that gossipy old biddy leaves."

"Annie! That's no way to talk about Mrs. Johnson."

Tommy stuck out his lower lip and huffed. "Grandpa called her that."

Cathy didn't argue. She sat on the other side of Tommy and stretched to hold both of them with one arm. Her eyes met Annie's and Cathy felt her first tears well up. Annie reached in front of Tommy for her grandmother's free hand. The three of them were still sitting quietly, tears flowing, when they heard Janet arrive.

Through the open window Edna's voice was clear. "Have they had Tony take the car away yet? They think it may have been suicide, you know. I told them he knew the road, knew better than to go fast on that curve. I was there when they were looking at the skid marks, heard them say he had to be going sixty straight for that tree when he started to brake. Poor man probably changed his mind at the last minute, but it was too late."

Annie tightened her grip on Cathy's hand.

I should have realized Annie heard the sheriff from here. Janet will get rid of Edna.

Janet tried. "Tony was just getting there. I can—"

Edna cut in to tell her story. "It was awful. I heard the crash and called 911—you know how many times someone's wrecked on that section of road. I thought I could help until the emergency crew got there, I did that before when that Smith girl hit a deer and was all shaken up. Well, I saw the car right away and it didn't look that bad, even though he'd run right into the tree. You know they built those old cars like tanks, not ready to crumple up like they do now. But he must not have been wearing a seat belt because he'd flown right over the windshield. His head had slammed into that tree, smashed like a pumpkin and the neck broken so it was flopping down, just awful, positively awful."

All three on the bed jerked at this description.

Cathy pulled the kids closer. *I'm an idiot. I should have closed the window.*

Janet cut the woman off before she could say more. "It was good of you to stay here and explain, but I'm sure you need to get home to make dinner. I'll stay as long as Cathy and the kids need me."

"Of course, dear, you are such a good friend. Suicide is so hard on those left behind."

And she'll want to get on the phone to tell everyone Henry killed himself.

Cathy blinked back tears.

Annie began to shake. "Suicide? Do you think he did that because we were so mad at him?"

Cathy shook her head. "No, Annie."

"What's suicide?" Tommy rubbed his fists against his eyes.

"It means he drove into the tree on purpose," sobbed Annie.

"We don't know he did that. It was probably an accident. Maybe a deer ran out in front of him." Cathy found herself hoping this was true, though the way he'd been on the phone, the paranoia, the nightmares—all of that made suicide seem likely.

But Annie picked up on her grandmother's words. "Remember, Tommy? All those deer crossing signs along the road?"

Cathy decided to build on Edna Johnson's example of the Smith girl. "Your mother ended up in the ditch along that same stretch of road, Tommy, when she was in high school. A deer ran out in front of her. We had to pull the car out with a tractor. It's lucky she didn't get hurt."

"I wish Grandpa'd been lucky."

"Me too." Cathy gave the kids a squeeze and stood up. She saw Edna's car leaving. "The gossipy old biddy's gone." She winked at Annie's small smile. "Let's go talk to Janet."

It could have been a deer.

***

The town's only mechanic stared at the underside of the Mercury while he prepared the car for towing. The sheriff's people were still at the scene.

"See any reason his brakes would have failed? Skid marks look like he pulled right to go off the road on purpose."

Tony kept his back to the voice, tightening up the hitch. He'd seen the skid marks, too. The brakes hadn't grabbed properly. "I've got to get it back to the shop and up on a lift to figure that out."

Once the Mercury was on the lift, Tony found the driver's side front bleeding nipple was loose enough to lose fluid and cause the car to veer right.

Off the road, into that tree. How could I have missed tightening it? I was rushing, but... Does anyone know I worked on the car this morning?

Tony considered what that kind of error could do to his insurance and business. He decided to simply say there'd been a brake failure, not surprising on such an old car. *An accident.*

Saturday morning, Steve Hillman stared at his mother across the breakfast table. "Where's Dave? I know you've talked with him. Stop protecting him."

She took a sip of her morning tea and stared back at him silently.

"Did he do this?" Steve pointed to the headline on the weekend edition of the town paper—*Local Man Dead in Tragic Accident.* They still got the paper edition for his mother, who insisted no one over ninety should have to use a computer.

She shrugged, an action barely discernible inside the fuzzy pink robe that had fit well twenty years earlier, when she was three inches taller and many pounds heavier. "What does it matter? If he did, it's only fair."

"Henry covered for Dave when he went AWOL."

She spit on her plate. "He was the reason your brother went AWOL. In a jungle filled with gooks! They captured your brother and tortured him for months. My Davey did die."

"I guess he did. The man who came back is a blackmailer, maybe a murderer."

Her face had always hardened when one of her boys displeased her, but now it was full of hate as she glared at her younger son. "You need to support your brother. Without him, you'd have nothing."

"I'm ready to retire anyway." Steve folded the newspaper. "I'm not sure they'd bother taking action against me even if they were convinced I knew he wasn't dead when I used that money for school. And technically, you're the one who accepted the death benefit, knowing he was alive."

"Oh, so you'd throw your own mother under the bus?"

"You knew he wasn't dead. Henry said he told you."

"Well, he's not around to say so, is he." The old woman's face creased in a smile.

Steve's heart skipped a beat.

He did do something to Henry's car.

Monday afternoon Steve's cell phone rang while he was alone in his office.

"Hey, little brother. Lay off Mom and listen up. First of all, find out what Cathy Clark knows and whether Henry actually had anything that could hurt me."

"She doesn't know anything. The funeral is Wednesday, I have an appointment with her next week, Tuesday, to go over the will."

"You have the will? Does it mention an envelope she's never seen?"

"No, but there's a safety deposit box she didn't know about. It's probably there."

At that bank in Winton. "Can you get into it?"

"No, Cathy's the only one who'll be able to do that. I'll give her the key on Tuesday."

"If she doesn't have the key, I guess that can wait. I'll keep an eye on her, though. Now, the reason I came back in the first place was so you could repay me for your fine education and career. There's no retirement plan for the work I've done all my life."

"That's why you came back? Not for Henry?"

Dave snorted. "I hadn't thought of him for years, but seeing him in his perfect little life pissed me off. It was fun to torture him."

Steve took directions to deliver money the same way Henry had, but the blackmail didn't bother him as much as the possibility he was becoming an accessory to murder after the fact.

Or before? Were Cathy and her grandchildren safe?

He had less than a week to decide what he'd do.

Goodbyes

The Funeral

Sunlight glinted off the polished hardware of the simple casket next to the grave. Cathy stood stiffly between her grandchildren, each breath an effort in the humid heat. Henry had been gone for nearly a week. Once the body was released, the funeral director stopped insisting he could work wonders for an open casket. She would have opted for cremation, but Henry had confided long ago that he would rather feed worms than burn.

Cathy hadn't known what to say to people at the church. It took forever to shake hands and accept condolences after the service. Henry had written insurance policies for at least half the town. At the end, she asked Janet to stay in the parking lot to discourage anyone from impulsively following them to the private ceremony at the cemetery.

It had worked. Cathy and the children had the moment to themselves.

Once the minister finished saying prayers, they each put a flower on the casket, and Cathy herded the children away, before the box with their beloved grandfather was lowered into the ground by the men waiting a discrete distance away.

As they got to the car and Tommy slid into the back seat, Cathy's thoughts wandered to her own feelings. She still felt like part of her had been torn away with Henry's sudden death, but her sorrow was tempered by the knowledge that whatever had been haunting him couldn't hurt him anymore. He was finally at peace.

Having the kids to look after undoubtedly helped. They'd finally told her about the man at the carnival. Annie said she hadn't really seen him, but Grandpa had clearly been upset, it wasn't just Tommy. Cathy had talked to them about paranoia, but Tommy still insisted the man was bad.

Cathy's thoughts were interrupted by Annie.

She was still standing by the car door. "There's a man over there. Watching us."

Tommy's head jerked around to see through the back window. "It's not him."

Cathy turned to look. He was up by the tree line, but she recognized Rob.

"It's okay, Annie. It's an old friend of Grandpa's." Cathy leaned into the car and turned the key one click in the ignition. "Put your windows down." She lowered the front ones. You kids wait here. I'll only be a minute."

She met the solitary figure halfway to the trees and touched his arm. "Rob, I'm so glad you're here." The decades melted away. "I thought I'd see you at the church."

"I didn't want to intrude." Rob nodded toward the graveside, from which they were being watched. "We don't want to give them anything to talk about."

Cathy dropped her hand. "Sometimes I hate living in a small town."

They walked toward her car with a proper space between them, meandering around graves and their markers respectfully.

"Your grandkids?" He nodded toward the car.

"Yes. They're living with us this summer while Tina's working overseas."

"She's not here now?"

Cathy had answered this repeatedly today. "No. She would have had to fly right back again. Ten hours each way. I told her it was okay not to come. And even though it was the middle of the night for Tina, Annie used my phone to let her be at the funeral virtually."

Tears started pouring silently down Cathy's face. "Henry would be glad you're here." Cathy paused and snuffled. "Please, walk slower. I don't want the kids to see me like this."

"It's okay." Rob started to reach for her, but abruptly pulled his hand back before she noticed. "It's okay to cry now."

"He hurt so much. The nightmares came back a couple weeks ago."

"I know. Janet told me."

"He'd been better for years. Why now?" Cathy sobbed.

"You know Henry always felt guilty—he was the one who got drafted—and now he had you, a daughter, grandchildren, everything. A life. A full life."

Cathy stopped and stared at Rob, oblivious to the twinge of envy in his voice. "That's it. It has to be. He was about to retire. We had so many plans, then the nightmares came back and he changed his mind and kept working. Guilt. That makes so much sense. God, I wish he had been willing to talk to someone."

"Janet wanted me to make the first move. I said no, but I kept thinking of ways to start... then it was too late." Rob's throat constricted. "I'm so sorry."

Understanding flowed through Cathy. "He didn't—I know what people are saying—but the sheriff said it was an accident. Bad brakes."

Rob gave a sigh of relief. "That's good to know."

"They gave out on that hairpin curve on the way to our house. We have the old Randall place, up on the hill."

"It's pretty out there."

They resumed walking at a sedate pace, side by side but not touching. It felt right.

"Where were you all these years?" Cathy glanced at Rob. He was wearing jeans and an ironed cotton shirt. His hair was still mostly brown. *He's aged well.*

"Cleaned up. Got a life. Went to school. Taught art and photography until I could retire and actually set myself up as a photographer."

Cathy laughed. "Okay, you've practiced that answer."

Rob nodded. "At least six times a day the first few weeks back here."

"Did you ever marry? Have kids?"

He shook his head. "I never let it get that serious."

Cathy looked ahead at her grandchildren waiting in the car. Rob had always wanted to be a father. *You should have had children. But I can't say that.* "Henry missed you. When they were planning your thirty-year class reunion, they came to him to find out where the other Musketeer was. He felt bad that he had no idea. No one did."

"The Three Musketeers." Rob smiled and glanced over at her. "Remember when Henry grabbed that bottle of Jack Daniels from my dad's liquor cabinet?"

Cathy smiled. "Rudy caught us all drinking under the bleachers."

Rob laughed. "God, I'd forgotten Rudy. He was a crazy old coot, stumbling around town drunk all the time."

"He froze to death years ago."

Rob shook his head at the unfortunate end. "Remember? We shared the bottle with him, and when he found out it was my parents' booze, he said he'd break in and steal some more. I didn't sleep for a week."

"Well, he wasn't the one Henry was afraid of." The words popped out of her mouth without thought.

"Henry was afraid?" Rob's light tone was gone, replaced by serious concern. "Janet only said he was having nightmares and acting weird."

Cathy sighed. *We were talking about old times and I brought it back to Henry's paranoia. May as well finish what I started.*

"He got obsessive about having the house locked up tight at night. Now the kids told me there was a man at the July 4th carnival that Henry seemed afraid of. I suppose that's who had him paranoid again." She stepped farther away from Rob as they reached the car. "Thanks for listening."

Rob held out a business card. "Call me if you want to talk some more."

"Thanks." Cathy put it into her pocket without a glance. *I've already said more than I should have.*

She got into the stifling hot car. "Seat belts on?"

Both children said yes. With a raised hand and nod, Cathy bid Rob farewell and started the car. Before driving away, she glanced back at her husband's gravesite. They were starting to fill the hole.

He'd feel so trapped. But he's not in that body anymore. He's free.

"I'm hot. Can we go swimming?"

Tommy's plea jarred her for a moment. Cathy glanced back. Both kids were sweaty. She cranked the AC and headed home. For a few minutes, she'd almost felt normal talking with Rob, remembering old times, catching up. Normal was a good thing. If someone wanted to judge her for playing with her grandchildren today, let them be damned. Besides, no one would see them at the creek.

"Sure we can go swim."

The Creek

At home, the children ran straight to their rooms to put on their suits. Cathy looked at the papers on the dining room table—insurance policies, IRA statements, a copy of Henry's will. She whisked them into an envelope. *That can all wait.*

"Grandma? You said we could go swimming." Tommy was already in his swim shorts.

"Yes. Give me a minute to change."

"Can we have some of those cookies Mrs. Johnson brought over? She's a pretty good cook for a snoop."

"Tommy!"

"Grandpa said she was a snoop."

"None of us should call her a snoop."

Tommy's face suddenly fell. His chest heaved once and he looked up at Cathy with shiny eyes. "I'm gonna miss Grandpa."

"Oh, Tommy," Cathy crouched and drew him to her in a rocking hug. "Me, too."

Annie walked into the room, dropped her towel, and joined the tearful embrace.

"Well." Cathy snuffled a few minutes later. "It's a hot day. Do you guys still want to swim? I don't think Grandpa would want us to huddle inside crying all day."

The children nodded soddenly.

"Have some of Mrs. Johnson's cookies while I change."

Cathy put on cut-offs and a T-shirt and immediately felt lighter.

Henry would approve. He was never much for formality.

The kids ran ahead of her once they got to the woods. When Cathy caught up they were playing in the long shallow section where the water slowed to form a pool for swimming. She stood on the bank watching them.

"Look!" Tommy rolled onto his back and made his way the whole length.

His sister bragged for him. "He doesn't need to touch bottom anymore. Since you're with us, can we go to the deep swimming hole? I like sliding down the waterfall."

Tommy chimed in. "I want to try, now I swim good. I can doggie paddle some, too, but mostly I look up and go on my back."

Cathy laughed. "Fine, but no running ahead."

They went at Cathy's careful pace along the rocky creek bed to the swimming hole. Annie was a pretty good swimmer. Tommy reminded Cathy of a crayfish, wiggling his hands and feet to move backwards with his face to the sky. Both children loved sliding down the short waterfall into the pool. Cathy got hot watching them and slipped into the chilly water briefly. As she dried in the sun, she relaxed for the first time since July 4th. *Whatever was going on, Henry's at peace now. I should do that National Park tour with the kids. Enjoy the summer. After Tina's home, I can decide how to move on with my life.*

Fortunately, the children got hungry right when Cathy was thinking they should be done. While they walked back through the woods, they talked about good times with Henry. They were all laughing as they crossed the road and Edna Johnson pulled out of the driveway.

The woman stopped and spoke through her open window. "I brought some cold ham and macaroni salad over, dear. I thought you might not feel up to cooking."

"Thank you, that was very thoughtful of you." Cathy smiled.

"Yes," drawled Edna. She stared disapprovingly at Cathy's wet, clinging clothes and the children in their swimsuits with towels draped over their shoulders. "I put it in that little refrigerator on your porch."

"Thank you so much. Annie, run right up and put it inside in the good refrigerator. That old one doesn't work very well. We only use it for cold drinks in the summertime."

"So I noticed," replied Edna coldly as the children scampered up the hill. "Well, I have to be going, dear. I still have my own supper to fix."

Cathy started up the driveway. Another car pulled in and stopped beside her.

Janet leaned out her window, head tilted back, and drawled "Yes" as she scanned Cathy from toe to head, a disapproving look on her face.

The imitation of Edna Johnson made Cathy giggle hysterically. She spoke between hiccups of laughter. "Oh Janet, the kids were hot and I decided to swim and that woman saw us come out of the woods laughing, and she'd left food in Henry's beer fridge. It's still full. She'll tell everyone I'm boozing it up and don't give a hoot about my poor departed husband." The laughter dissolved into sobs. "And she probably thinks that I'm too old to wear cut-offs, too."

"She's not that much older than us, but yeah, I don't think she ever wore cut-offs. Get in. I'll drive you up to the house."

"I'll get your seat wet."

"Won't hurt this old thing."

Cathy nodded soggily and got into the passenger seat. "We miss him, Janet. I miss him. But I was so scared he wasn't going to get better this time."

"I know. At the funeral, Steve mentioned how tense Henry was last week. Oh, we made an appointment for you next Tuesday—figured you could use a few days before going over the money stuff."

"Thanks."

The Yearbook

When they got to the house, Annie was setting the table for dinner. "Tommy's hungry. I figured we could eat some of the food people brought over."

"Sure," said Cathy. "Let's put everything out on the counter buffet style and we can microwave anything that needs heat... Janet, you'll join us?"

"Sure."

Tommy filled his plate with lasagna and meatballs in some kind of gravy. Cathy considered telling him to balance that out with one of the salads or some fruit, but decided this one day he could eat whatever he felt like. He surprised her by getting watermelon instead of cookies when he went back for seconds.

He started to raise the slice to his mouth, then stopped. "That guy at the cemetery was a friend of Grandpa's?"

Janet apologized. "I'm sorry. I thought I kept everyone back."

"It was Rob. He watched from a distance. We talked a bit after."

"Who is he?" demanded Tommy.

"We all went to school together. Rob was best man at our wedding."

Annie shook her head. "I never saw him in your wedding pictures."

"Sure you have. The one with long hair."

Annie went and got the photo from the living room. "The hippie next to Grandpa? He looks better with short hair. Did he have long hair like that in school, too?"

"No. That was not allowed. I think I can find our old yearbooks. I'll show you later." *It will be nice to remember the good times, before everyone changed.*

After dinner, they cleaned up the kitchen together, then took a long walk and watched the sunset. As they got back to the house, Annie reminded Cathy about the yearbook.

"I'll leave you to it." Janet pulled out her car keys. "Just don't look at my pictures!"

"Kids, get ready for bed and I'll find a yearbook."

As they ran into the house, Cathy walked Janet to her car.

Janet paused before opening her door. "So, how did it go with Rob?"

Cathy shrugged. "It was nice. He's still easy to talk to."

"You were always good together."

Cathy gave Janet a sour look. "We were talking. Period. I just buried my husband today."

Janet flinched. "I know. I'm sorry."

"Besides, we were teenagers, Jan. We're not the same people."

Cathy waved as Janet drove away, then went into the house to find the yearbooks. *Henry's senior year is the one they'll want to see.*

Cathy dug it out of a box in her closet, then went and curled up on Tommy's bed between the two children. "This is the year your grandpa and Rob and Janet graduated. I was a year behind them." She leafed through the pages. "Here's Grandpa's picture."

Tommy looked surprised. "He looks like a kid."

"He was, Tommy. Eighteen is still a kid."

"Where's your picture?" Annie touched the page.

Cathy flipped back to the junior class. "Here I am. How do you like that hair style?"

"You're prettier now."

"Thanks." Cathy searched through the pages. "This is what I wanted you to see. Your Grandpa, Rob, and Dave. We used to call them the Three Musketeers because they were always together, all the way through school, and they all went into the service together when they graduated."

"What happened to the other guy?" Tommy pointed at the picture.

Cathy paused. She decided to give the simplest, direct answer. "He died in the war."

"Dave. That's who Grandpa hollered for at night!" Annie reached for the book.

Cathy let her take it. *So they did hear his nightmares. At least they weren't as scared as Tina was when she was little.*

Annie leafed through the book, asking questions. The picture of Rob and Cathy as prom king and queen set off some discussion.

"So you dated one Musketeer in high school, then ended up with another." Annie smirked. "Mom's already talked to me about not thinking every boy I date is 'the one.' I guess she's right. Can I keep the book to look at?"

"Sure. Now let's connect with your mom."

They had their virtual visit with Tina, talked about Henry, and cried some more.

When the kids were finally settled, Cathy stood staring sightlessly at the living room. Henry was really gone. He wasn't just late coming home. She shivered a little. She was on her own now. Janet was her only close friend. Others had drifted away over the years, some early on when Henry was still moody, most of them busy starting families long before they finally had Tina. Cathy's reflection was interrupted by the peal of her cell phone.

"Hello?"

"Hi, it's Rob. Janet gave me your number. I hope it's okay to call."

I told her it's too soon for her matchmaking.

Cathy realized she was making the rounds, locking up the way Henry had been insisting, and stopped. She opened a window to let the evening breeze cool the room.

Rob talked in her silence. "I just wanted to make sure you're okay. The landline wasn't working."

His voice was comforting.

I don't need to be rude. "I'm okay so far. It's a little spooky out here, knowing Henry won't be home."

"You're all alone?"

"The kids are in bed." She moved from window to window, letting in the air.

"I could come out if you want company."

"No, don't!" *Edna Johnson's probably watching the road.*

"I'm sorry. I didn't mean..."

"Don't worry about it." She stared at the deadbolt on the front door. *With the windows open, it's silly to lock the door. Or should I go back and lock the windows?*

Rob's voice broke through her thoughts. "It's just... I'm worried about you. I know it's been difficult. Janet..."

"Henry was a good man." Cathy slid the deadbolt into place.

"I know."

"A good husband and a good father." She moved back to close and lock the windows.

"Of course he was. I didn't mean to imply he wasn't."

"Well, thanks for calling."

"I'm here if you need me."

Cathy hung up, then finished checking that all the windows and doors were locked up for the night. Rob didn't seem like the angry drunk she'd turned away, but he wasn't the boy she'd dated in high school, either.

She remembered what he said about the landline and checked it. No dial tone. She followed the cord and realized it had been unplugged. *How did that happen?*

She plugged it back in and checked the dial tone was working.

***

Dave slid into his sleeping bag in the back of his pickup, parked in the woods above the Clark home on an old logging road accessed from the adjacent property. Once they were settled for the night, he'd put a listening device in Cathy's car.

Thanks to an open window, he'd been able to get into the house while they were at the funeral. He hadn't found anything disturbing but he had bugged the kitchen. He'd been in the orchard listening all evening.

I should have put one upstairs. The lights in the bedrooms had stayed on for quite a while after Janet left.

Cathy said she was going to show them our yearbook.... *Nah, the kids would never recognize me from those photos.*

He stared up at the stars.

So Rob went radical hippie when he got back. Figures. That explains how she ended up with Henry. Cathy was always pretty square. Bet that was Rob who called her tonight.

Dave had watched her locking the windows.

How much did Henry tell you, Cathy?

Tommy's Nightmare

"No!" screamed Tommy.

Cathy woke up as her feet hit the floor. The first digit on her clock was a two.

Tommy's room was right across the hall, his door open. Light from the bathroom provided faint illumination. He'd screamed himself awake and was lying there, eyes wide, petrified. Cathy sat down beside him and ran a soothing hand along his face.

"It was just a bad dream, sweetheart."

Tommy stared at his grandmother, then curled up around her. "It was the bad man. The man from the carnival. The bald man with black eyes and the shark smile."

The man from the carnival. Annie didn't seem to think he was anything to worry about. But Cathy let Tommy keep talking.

"Grandpa told me to watch out for him, that he was a bad man and I should tell if I ever saw him. I figured out the man's why Grandpa didn't want us to camp in the yard."

Oh God, Henry and his paranoia.

"There is no bad man, Tommy. Grandpa was joking with you." *Dammit, Henry, why did you scare our grandson with this?*

But Tommy was determined. "There is too. He bumped Grandpa hard."

"Bumping into someone doesn't make you bad." She gently stroked Tommy's arm.

He yanked it away. "No. The man stared right at Grandpa, then smiled. It was scary."

"Why would that be scary? I'm sure it was just an accident."

"No!" Tommy insisted. "There was lots of room. He ran into Grandpa on purpose, and his smile *was* scary. His eyes didn't smile with his mouth. Annie didn't see his face. That's why she made it sound not important when we told you."

Tommy was so solemn giving these details, Cathy began to wonder what had really happened. "Grandpa told you he was afraid of this man?"

"Not exactly. But Grandpa told me I should tell him right away if I ever saw that man again. He said not to say anything to you or Annie, 'cause we didn't want you to be scared."

"And Annie didn't see him?"

"Not really. She didn't see his face."

"Well..." Cathy's mind raced. *Did Henry think the man was a pedophile? No. He would have told me. Maybe Tommy told Henry the man had scared him, and Henry was trying to reassure him. That has to be it.* "Grandpa didn't tell me anything about that man, so I don't think it was too serious, but if you see him around here, you tell me. Okay?"

"Okay."

"And the house is locked up tight for the night, just like Grandpa liked it to be."

The Letters

The home office had sent Thomas to represent them at Henry's funeral, then stay over and clean out the office the next day. They were going to let this branch go, since more and more business was being done online. Thursday morning, Thomas sorted through the paperwork on Henry's desk.

There were envelopes ready to mail and proposals waiting for meetings or to be mailed. Thomas decided to phone all involved parties before sending out anything. He started by opening the ones ready to mail carefully, so they could be sent in the original envelope if appropriate.

On each call, he explained Henry had passed and that this office would be closing. He found most people had been at the funeral and wanted to talk about how wonderful Henry had been. They weren't happy about the office closing but were reassured somewhat when Thomas promised to enclose his own business card with their information. They would still have someone to call directly.

At the end of the day, Thomas found two more addressed envelopes in the bottom desk drawer, separate from the others—one thin and the other quite bulky—with a sticky note on top: Personal. Mail if anything happens to me. Given the circumstances of Henry's death and the chatter he'd heard at the funeral, Thomas was tempted to read them. He looked at the sticky note again. Personal. *Not my business.*

Henry had used plain envelopes, not the ones with the company address printed on them. Thomas debated adding a return address, but the office one would be useless and if Henry was mailing these from here, they might be something he wouldn't have wanted his wife to see. Thomas decided to mail them as Henry had left them. If the addresses were no good, they would end up in the dead letter bin at the post office.

It's Complicated

Church

The Sunday after Henry's funeral, Janet checked to see who all was in church. When her eyes reached the opposite pew, they met Rob's. He gave a sheepish half-smile and a shrug. Janet smiled back warmly, her eyes dancing. He didn't ordinarily come to church and had resisted her suggestion that he start—what more proper atmosphere in which to see a newly bereaved widow without making her feel pursued? Rob and Cathy were Janet's best friends. She didn't want them to miss their chance to be together. Of course it was too soon, but when Cathy was ready, she'd know Rob was there.

Cathy joined Janet and glanced over to see where she had been looking. Cathy gave Rob a brief polite smile and turned to give Janet a warning glare.

Janet tried to look innocent.

During the sermon, Cathy found her mind wandering. She was surprised she found herself instantly taking comfort from Rob's presence, the same as she had at the cemetery.

I don't need to feel guilty about that. He was best man at our wedding and there hasn't been anything romantic between us since long before Henry and I started dating. He's probably feeling bad he wasn't there for Henry all this time, and he's worried for me now.

She glanced over at Rob. He was facing forward, seemingly focused on the service, but Edna Johnson sat beyond him and locked eyes with Cathy briefly.

Great. Cathy fleetingly envied widows in the days of formal mourning, when each stage of adjustment had its recognized rituals and taboos and a specific time limit. Edna Johnson wasn't the only one to seem disapproving. Several other ladies from church had brought food and found her playing with the kids. *We'll take the last of it to Suzie's this afternoon.*

Cathy's sister had insisted they come, because she had been helping her son after emergency surgery and hadn't been able to drive in for the funeral. As much as her older sister annoyed Cathy with her bossiness, getting away from the house for the night would be nice. Cathy kept expecting Henry to be there.

She pretended to concentrate on the service, but in reality she was mentally listing what had to be done before she and the kids left for her sister's. She hoped Suzie wouldn't talk negatively about Henry or his mental health. *Thank God the sheriff decided it was an accident. But at least Suzie will understand why I'm not crying uncontrollably all day.*

At the end of the service, Cathy tried to slip out quickly, but people kept stopping to offer their condolences before she could get out of the pew.

"I'll get the kids," Janet offered. "We'll meet you on the steps."

It seemed to take forever, but at last Cathy got out the door and spotted the children with Janet—and Rob. Cathy hesitated before walking over to them.

There's Edna Johnson and all her friends, and all the people who just offered me condolences. This does not look good. But if I just wave for the kids to come to me, that will look like I'm hiding something. This sucks!

She walked over and kept the children between her and the two adults.

"Tommy was telling us his bike's broken," said Rob.

"He said the back tire's flat." Janet ruffled his hair and the little boy allowed it.

"I rode it in the woods. I know not to do that now "

"I told you not to before you did it." Annie was every bit an exasperated teenager.

"We've got a patch kit, a spare inner tube, and Henry's tools," Cathy explained. "But I'm not sure how to change it without messing up the derailleur." *I depended on Henry for so much.* "Is there anyone in town who does bike repairs?"

"I could fix it," offered Rob.

Janet chimed in. "Why don't Rob and I both come up when you get back from your sister's? We can have a picnic supper. I'll bring my potato salad and Rob makes dynamite zucchini bread."

Tommy looked up with his sweetest smile. He had chocolate on his face from the treats.

Cathy couldn't resist that smile. "I guess that would be okay. We'll be back late tomorrow afternoon." *At least anyone listening heard Janet suggest it and say they're both coming with food.*

"That's a short trip," said Rob.

"Suzie's only a couple hours away."

"I should be able to get out of work by four-thirty," Janet said. "We could be there by five or five-thirty?"

"Works for me," said Cathy.

"Five-thirty," said Rob. "I've got the studio open regularly now, until five."

They were about to leave when the pastor came up. Despite his seventy-some years, he moved energetically from group to group and seemed to know everyone by name.

"Rob, nice to see you in church. Cathy, how are you doing?" He took her hand as he asked.

Cathy felt his true concern. "Okay, thank you. Janet's been a great help, and Edna Johnson and some of the other ladies brought food to the house. I'm going to my sister's today."

"Oh, are you going to be gone long?"

"No, just overnight. I have to go over the will and everything with Steve Hillman Tuesday morning. And Rob and Janet are coming up tomorrow for dinner."

"And to fix my bike," Tommy inserted.

"Good, good," sanctioned the clergyman. "This is not a time to be alone too much. I'm glad you're holding up so well. Ah... excuse me, please. I wanted to speak to Mrs. Adams."

Cathy turned to Janet and Rob. "Well, we have to get going. We'll expect you about five-thirty tomorrow."

As Cathy headed to the car, she nodded to Edna Johnson, who was still on the steps chatting with friends. They were only a few years older than Cathy, but they were a judgmental bunch.

***

"Laughing," repeated Edna Johnson to the small group outside the church. "She'd just buried that poor man and there she was, soaking wet. Her hair looked like an old string mop that got tangled up. And all that beer in the refrigerator!"

She clucked her tongue. "Well, I don't know if this has driven her to drink or if she didn't give a hoot for that wonderful husband of hers. Why, just last winter, I was stuck in my driveway half a dozen times. And every time, Henry Clark stopped and pushed to help me. He usually came home the same time I get back from my volunteer work here at the church."

One of her friends nodded solemnly. "Well, you know, I just walked by them and she was inviting that Rob over for dinner tomorrow night. Invited Janet too, but you can't fool me. Now that is way too quick. And he's working his way in with the children, too, offering to fix the boy's bike."

Another woman spoke up. "Weren't they all good friends in school?"

"Maybe," Edna Johnson took control of the conversation again. "You know they're saying it was an accident now, but I was there and they thought at first it was suicide. Maybe she was carrying on already and that poor man knew it."

***

Dave was annoyed that he hadn't been able to get his hands on proper surveillance gear. He didn't want to be noticed in town. Wearing a hat might hide his scarred temple, but a hat would make a big stranger more memorable.

He had to watch from a distance while they were at church. Janet and Rob were easy to recognize when they came out with Cathy's grandkids. He'd listened in on their zoom visit with their mother the night before. So far, he hadn't heard anything of importance discussed in the car or kitchen, nothing about that damn envelope or the safety deposit box.

He saw Edna watch Cathy leave. The way she turned back to her friends was familiar—she'd always thought she was better than everyone else.

She was nice to me, though. The guys teased me about an older woman being after me. If it had been anyone else, I'd have eaten that up.

Home

Cathy was anxious to get on the road. Tommy and Annie were taking forever eating lunch at the kitchen table. "Come on you two, hurry it up!"

"You always tell me I eat too fast." Tommy took another bite.

"Finish your sandwich. Don't you want to see your cousins?" Cathy scanned the room for anything she'd forgotten. *I should have let them eat in the car.*

Tommy talked around the food in his mouth. "They're not real cousins."

Annie rolled her eyes. "Yes they are. Mom and their dad are cousins, so they're like our second cousins or something."

"At last! The silent one speaks!" Cathy smiled. "That's the first thing you've said since church, other than a grunt or two. Something bothering you?"

"Maybe. I'll talk about it when I have it straight in my mind."

"Okay. Meantime, can we pul-eeze get out of here? I wanted to be on the road a half hour ago."

Annie shoved back her chair. "Well don't blame us!" She flung her half-full paper plate into the trash, and stomped out of the room.

Cathy exchanged looks with Tommy. "I think I better go have a chat with your sister. Take your time finishing and leave us alone, okay?"

She found Annie lying on her stomach on her bed, hugging the panda bear from the carnival and crying with abandon. Cathy sat next to her and gingerly patted Annie's shoulders. "Hey, how about talking it out?"

Annie rolled to include her grandmother in her panda embrace. The sobbing slowly slackened. At last she could speak, with occasional snuffles and gulps. "You know how

Grandpa was getting so strange the last couple weeks? Like not wanting us to sleep in the yard when the cousins were here and stuff?"

Cathy nodded.

"I told him he was just like our dad and… I wished he'd go away, too, because he made you so worried all the time. And then he got killed… and I'm afraid God's punishing me for having those bad thoughts and maybe he'll take you away, too. Or Mom."

"No, Annie, no." Cathy pulled back enough to look at Annie eye to eye. "Your grandpa's accident had nothing to do with you."

Annie seemed to accept this assurance. She went on with the other matter on her mind. "And that guy, Rob? Grandpa didn't like him anymore, did he?"

Cathy took a deep breath while she decided how to answer. "They were friends growing up. I showed you, Rob was Grandpa's best man at our wedding. But they argued a lot about the war. Then Rob moved away and they never made up."

"You said he was your boyfriend in high school. I think he still likes you like that."

I guess if my granddaughter's picking up on it, I'm not imagining things. Cathy chose her words carefully. "You may be right. At least he may *think* he feels that way. But we broke up before they went to war, before your Grandpa and I started dating."

"What about you? And Grandpa? I heard Aunt Suzie saying you should get a divorce when she was here the last time."

Cathy felt the squeeze on her heart. *Life is so complicated, little girl.*

"I had no intention of taking that advice. I wanted your grandpa to get help, some kind of counseling, but I still loved him. Still do. I'm not done saying goodbye to him."

Annie nodded. "Me neither. Grandpa yelled for his friend who died. Did he see that happen? Is that why he had those nightmares and stuff?"

Cathy nodded. "I think so. He wouldn't talk about it."

Annie sighed. "When my kitten got run over, I saw that happen. It was awful. It was probably worse for Grandpa to see his friend die."

Cathy gave her a hug and wept. Then she pulled away to face Annie, blinking away the last tears.

We can't keep living in Henry's troubles. We have to let them rest, too.

"Grandpa does not want us to stop living. Let's go."

***

As soon as he heard Cathy in the kitchen talking about leaving, Dave moved his truck up the road from the driveway, so he could follow her. He remembered her sister Suzie. She'd been a lifeguard at the pool in town when they were twelve or so. *We all had the hots for her.*

When Cathy pulled into the driveway of a ranch house in an older suburb, he kept driving past a few more houses, then parked and watched in his rearview mirror. When Suzie bustled out to the car, she was wearing a tent-like dress.

So much for teenage idols.

It was clear from the packs coming out of the car that they'd be staying overnight. He drove around the block and was pleased to find Suzie's house was backed by a public park.

They're not going anywhere.

He went in search of dinner.

Visiting Suzie

Twenty years earlier, Suzie had ruled the social order in this neighborhood. Now in her eighties, she left that to others. She greeted Cathy and the kids wearing a muumuu. "The kids brought their swimsuits?"

"We're wearing them!" Tommy pointed to the trunks he was wearing for shorts.

Annie snapped the shoulder strap of her fluorescent pink suit.

"Go around to the back." Suzie waved at a gate. "My grandkids are in the pool."

"Where should they put their backpacks?" Cathy waved for the kids to grab their own bags.

"Just leave them on the picnic table. It's far enough from the pool to stay dry."

As the kids ran for the gate, Cathy asked, "Is anyone watching them?"

"Their father's back there. He can't move around much, but he can keep them in line yelling."

"His surgery went well then?"

"They say he'll be fine now. The stars must have been out of whack for our family, that and Henry happening so close together. Sorry I couldn't be there for you."

"Janet's been a rock and everyone's been giving us food." Cathy handed Suzie the box of leftovers. "I couldn't be here for you, either."

Suzie shrugged. "Joe's kids are older, and he didn't die. Come on in. I'll fix us a couple drinks."

Cathy grabbed her overnight bag and followed her sister to the kitchen, where Suzie went about making a pitcher of margaritas. They could hear shrieks of laughter from the backyard. Cathy peeked out and saw Suzie's son Joe in a lounge chair overseeing the antics in the pool. Joe Jr., his oldest, was demanding Tommy prove he could swim across the pool without stopping or touching before he'd let him into the deep end.

"They'll be fine. Joe Jr. just took lifesaving. He'll probably be working as a guard next summer." Suzie handed Cathy a salt-rimmed drink. "You're in the chin-up, everything will work out stage, aren't you?"

"I guess. It isn't quite real yet. I keep expecting him to come home."

Suzie got her own margarita and motioned for Cathy to sit at the kitchen table. "How's Tina handling it?"

"She's okay. You can talk with her tonight. She always video chats with the kids before they go to bed. Annie did something like that at the funeral, on my phone, with Tina. She's got at least four more weeks over there."

"Then you'll be alone."

The reality hit Cathy. "Yeah. I'll be alone then. Unless Janet has her way."

"She wants to move in with you?" Suzie snorted her disbelief.

"No. Do you remember Rob Harris?"

"Of course I remember him. He was your sexy boyfriend who was always so nice. I never could understand why you preferred Henry."

Cathy bristled. "Don't you remember what he was like when he came home?"

"Who? Henry or Rob? Oh, Henry was alright. I don't want to offend you, but he was so... boring." Suzie waved her hand dismissively.

"You say that as if it's a slimy sort of thing." *Why did I start this conversation?*

"He sold insurance, Cath..." Suzie stopped herself. "Shit. I'm sorry. You're right. He was a steady, dependable guy once he got past that PTSD. But it was coming back, wasn't it? Wasn't that why he freaked out about the kids camping in the yard?"

"I don't want to talk about Henry with you." Cathy took a long sip of her drink.

"Fair enough."

They sat quietly a few moments.

Suzie thought back to Cathy's original question. "Why did you ask if I remembered Rob?"

"He showed up at the cemetery, stood back so I didn't see him until we were leaving. I hadn't seen him since the wedding, but it was so easy talking with him, I could relax and be myself."

"Uh-huh." Suzie nodded her head knowingly. "I'd forgotten that shouting match we all heard. I was watching you. I wasn't sure whether you'd go through with the wedding to Henry or slip away with Rob."

"Baloney. Rob was drunk, as usual. I was just worried he'd make another scene at the wedding."

"Yeah, sure." Suzie took a sip of her drink. "So, is he married or anything?"

"No. And Janet? She's trying to be subtle, but you know Janet. She gave him my cell number and then this morning she introduced him to the kids at church, and Rob offered to fix Tommy's bike, and all of a sudden they're coming to dinner tomorrow. Even Annie picked up on the fact Rob still has feelings for me."

"His feelings and Janet's matchmaking are not what's bothering you, sis." Suzie stared at Cathy, waiting for her to reach the obvious conclusion herself. It worked.

"It's too soon. I should only be feeling sorrow for Henry." Cathy looked down at her hands on the table.

"What did you tell Annie?"

Cathy shrugged. "We agreed neither of us is done saying goodbye to Henry."

"So be friends—for now." Suzie drained her glass and stood up. "Let's get you settled."

***

When Dave came back from eating, he found a place where he could leave the truck overnight. Then he hiked across the park with a small listening device and was pleased to find a grove of trees from which he could see and hear Cathy and Suzie in the backyard. The sun had just set.

They'll never notice me here. I wonder what conversation I missed. Should have eaten at a drive-thru.

***

Suzie's son and his boys had left and the pool wasn't as much fun without them.

"Aunt Suzie, can we watch some television?"

"Sure, but rinse off and put your pajamas on first."

As they ran into the house, Cathy laughed. "That's the fastest they've followed directions all day."

"Except when Joe Jr. was ordering them around." Suzie got up. "Do you want another margarita?"

"I think there's only enough for one left in the pitcher. You go ahead and have it. I'm pretty buzzed as it is." Cathy leaned her head back. "It's nice you have the park behind you. It's dark enough to see stars."

"And the peepers will be serenading us any moment now." Suzie shut the door when she returned, closing off the faint sounds of children and television. She handed Cathy a bottle of water and settled in with her own drink.

The two women sat without talking for several minutes.

Cathy broke the silence, speaking quietly. "I think maybe Henry... they said it was an accident, but he always drove that road slowly... they said he was going too fast for the curve..."

"There's probably no way to be sure, from what you told me before."

"No. But I wonder if I shouldn't have done more... I mean, I tried to get him to go talk to someone. Maybe I should have told him you thought I should divorce him. Maybe if he'd thought he might lose me he would have agreed to counseling. I just don't know." She choked on her tears. "I can't help but feel I should have found some way to help him, that there was something else I could have done. I keep going over it, trying to figure out a way to convince him. And I keep imagining him saying 'Okay Honey, if you feel that strongly about it, I'll go see someone.' Or—"

"Knock it off." Suzie snapped at her sister. "Stop playing the guilt game. Even if it was suicide, you did your best, Cathy. If you'd tried harder to make him get help, he might have felt you were pushing him away and become more desperate. You will never know. Accept the past and deal with today."

"Yes ma'am." Cathy smiled weakly. "Thanks for the lecture."

"No problem. That's what big sisters are for... Are you going to be okay financially?"

"I've always had my own money from teaching, and the retirement now, but Henry handled everything else."

Suzie gave her a disapproving look.

Cathy put her hand up defensively. "I know, but he liked taking care of the bills and all those details. And... okay, it was easier... I've got an appointment on Tuesday with Steve Hillman. He's always handled our financial and legal stuff. We'll go over the will and everything else."

***

Dave smiled.

It doesn't sound like Henry told her anything. But that safety deposit box... once she gets in there, I'll have to get rid of her. Steve needs to give me that key. If she doesn't know about it now, why does she ever need to? But if it was abandoned, someone would eventually open it. There's got to be a way for me to get into it.

Monday, July 25, 2022

Janet's Errand

Janet typed an investment summary for Mr. Rubish.

She caught herself adding an extra 'b' to his name and shook her head angrily. She'd have to spell check for that on everything she did for him.

Steve was on the phone in the inner office.

Ordinarily, they had a good working relationship. He treated her more like a co-worker than an employee. But the last several days had been miserable. He said he was having some personal financial problems. He'd protected half the town, guiding them to safe investment options and sound legal decisions. *Sad he's not doing as well for himself.*

"Janet!"

His tone did not sit well with her, but she got up and entered his office without delay.

"Go to my house and get the Wilson folio immediately!"

He was biting her head off because he'd left papers at home!

"Yes, sir!" clipped Janet, turning sharply to leave.

"What? Oh, I'm sorry."

Janet turned back to him. "What's wrong?"

"I told you. I made some bad investments for myself and I'm feeling the pinch."

He avoided looking at her as he spoke.

That was not like Steve, either. *Oh well, if he doesn't want to talk about it, I can't force it out of him.* She spoke in a soothing tone. "I'll go over as soon as I finish that report for Mr. Rubish. Then you'll have it if he comes in while I'm gone."

"How long will that take?"

"Oh, fifteen or twenty minutes."

"No!" He was barking out words again. "I don't want you to wait that long. Go get those papers right now. Mr. Rubish isn't due until this afternoon. If he comes early again, it's his own problem."

"Okay, you're the boss."

It didn't make sense, though. The Wilsons wouldn't be back until later in the week. Janet shook off her puzzlement. If Mr. Rubish had to wait, it wouldn't be her fault.

She stopped at the ladies' room that she shared with the women who worked in the dentist's office.

A young girl was rehearsing in the mirror. "I know I don't have much experience... No, I haven't really worked anywhere, but I just got out of school... Oh!" the girl blushed. "I didn't hear the door open. I was practicing. It's my first real job interview. I'm a little nervous."

"I don't blame you," soothed Janet. "What's the job?"

"Dr. Gunner, the dentist. He's hiring a receptionist who can do some secretarial work." The girl sighed. "I'm just afraid he won't hire me. I've got secretarial training and I took bookkeeping in high school, but I've never worked anywhere, except one summer I was a clerk in a shoe store."

Janet put a hand on her shoulder. "Let me give you a hint. Say it positively. Instead of 'I've never... except' say 'I have both secretarial training and experience dealing with the public.' Can you give someone at the shoe store as a reference?"

"Oh yes, they were very happy with my work, I just want a job that will use my training."

"That makes sense. Remember you're selling yourself now. Be positive pointing out your good points. He'll probably know what weaknesses to expect from your written application. Don't emphasize them by bringing them up yourself."

"I know you're right. I guess I'm just so nervous, I wasn't thinking. Thanks." The girl smiled. "I better get going or I'll start by being late. Thanks again."

Janet made hurried use of the facilities, then started down the stairs. There was an elevator, but she liked the exercise.

A man was on his way up.

Janet smiled briefly in passing, but was focused on her errand and didn't really pay attention to the large bald man.

***

Half an hour later, Janet checked the time on her cell phone impatiently. Mr. Rubish was sure to come in before she finished his report. She had wasted time in the ladies' room, plus more driving across town to the Hillman home, now this. *What is taking Mrs. Hillman so long?*

The elderly woman had been adamant that Janet stay by the front door, but she was taking forever. Janet took a few steps down the hallway toward the back of the house and called to Steve's mother. "Are you sure you don't want some help? I know exactly what it looks like. I could probably find it in a jiffy."

"No, no! You mustn't come back here and see this disaster. I haven't had time to clean today and it gets so messy over the weekend with Stevie home. I can't really do anything while he's here."

Janet waited a few more minutes with her intolerance for the house-proud old woman growing. At last she headed down the hall, wanted or not.

"Really," she placated Mrs. Hillman, "You're much too harsh on yourself. My house rarely looks this good and I live alone! Now let me find that file."

Visibly flustered, the elderly woman stepped back and watched Janet leaf through papers on the desk. Mrs. Hillman glanced surreptitiously at a wall clock.

Janet was annoyed. Not only was the house immaculate, but the folio she needed was right in the middle of the desk, clearly labeled. It shouldn't have taken anyone twenty minutes to find the file—and Steve's mother hadn't found it at all. Janet tried to sound pleasant. "Here it is."

"Oh, you are so quick!" Mrs. Hillman moved closer, trapping Janet behind the desk. "I always say my Stevie has a smart girl working for him. That shows he's smart, too. Some mothers don't like to brag about their children. I figure they don't have anything to brag about!"

"Maybe not," said Janet. Mrs. Hillman showed no sign of moving out of her way. "I really need to get this back to the office."

"Oh, I'm sure you could stay for a cup of tea."

"I really do need to go." Since Mrs. Hillman didn't move, Janet edged sideways trying to get past her. Brushing against the desk, she knocked a book to the floor. She bent down to pick it up. *A Beginner's Guide to Automotive Repair?* "Is Steve doing his own repair work?"

She looked up to see a stricken look on Mrs. Hillman's face.

"Oh, no. No, that's something I took out of the library myself. Curiosity. Stevie doesn't know a thing about cars. I thought maybe I could do some small things on my own vehicle, to save him the expense. I don't like being a burden to him. But I'm afraid I was silly to think I could do any of that at my age." The elderly woman gave a helpless shrug and a nervous smile.

"Is Steve really in financial trouble?"

"No, dear, it's just he worries about it all the time. You know, his father was like that, always worried we'd be poor again. We were, terribly poor, when we were children, in Europe, after the war."

"I'd really love to talk, but I have to get back to work."

"Stevie could spare you a little longer. Are you sure you don't want some tea?" Mrs. Hillman was still blocking Janet's exit.

Janet shook her head. "I wanted to finish work early because I'm having dinner out at Cathy Clark's house. I'll be lucky to leave on time if I head back right now."

Mrs. Hillman glanced at the wall clock and finally stepped aside. "That poor girl. How is she doing?"

"Okay, considering." Janet strode past the woman. "I'll let myself out. Have a good day."

Janet started her car and tried to let go of her irritation.

Am I going to be like that in a few years, desperate for company? At least Mrs. Hillman has her son living with her. Maybe I'm lucky I still need to work.

***

Mrs. Hillman watched Janet drive away, then spoke into the phone with her voice full of urgency. "She just left. I couldn't hold her any longer. Is he gone?"

Her younger son answered. "Yes. She saw him on his way up the stairs, but she didn't seem to recognize him. I don't think there's any need to worry."

"You don't worry about anything, Stevie."

"Mother, don't get yourself so upset. If she did think she recognized him, she wouldn't believe it."

"Maybe."

"He took the key. I told him they won't let him in the box, but he insisted. He shouldn't have come here. He should leave. I can send him money if that's what he wants."

"Does Davey know it was her on the stairs?"

"Yes, Mother. But I told him, she'd have reacted if she recognized him. There's nothing to worry about."

She hung up.

Actually, Steve was worried. Banks always gave you two keys for a safety deposit box. Hopefully his brother didn't know that, or that Cathy's name on the box meant the bank would be in touch with her eventually, even if Steve didn't tell her about it.

Anticipation

Rob adjusted the lighting. He'd rather take dozens of informal shots to capture the one moment that really displayed the essence of a person, but formal portraits did more to augment his retirement. At least these two children were well-behaved—though they were of course terribly curious about all his lights and technical gizmos.

"What's that?" asked the nine-year-old girl.

"A light meter. It tells me how much light there is so I know how much to add and how to adjust the shutter speed on the cameras."

"How come you have two cameras set up?" Her little brother asked.

"Your parents want some pictures in black and white and some in color. That's two different kinds of film, so two different cameras."

"Isn't it easier to just take the picture with your phone?" The girl looked puzzled.

"Yes, but this will give us better photos."

"Stop pestering the man," said their mother. "If you want to have time to go to the playground after this."

Rob smiled. While he didn't like portraits, he did like working with children. As he arranged these two and took their photos, he thought of Tommy and Annie. He already had his toolbox in the truck so he'd be able to fix Tommy's bike tonight.

He hoped Cathy was okay with his coming over. Janet had kind of pushed them all into this picnic—but he did go to church hoping for a chance to see Cathy. He wanted her to remember he was there, so she wouldn't turn to anyone else, but he didn't want to rush her, either. He'd have to play it by ear. *I don't want to lose her again.*

***

Cathy pulled into the driveway, glad to be home.

They couldn't find Annie's cell phone when it was time to leave, then the kids had been quarrelsome in the car over nothing in particular. Before he unlatched his seatbelt, Tommy asked if they could go to the creek.

"No," Cathy snapped. "You went swimming before we left and were awful all the way home."

Tommy thrust out his lower lip and ran off behind the house.

"He's going to pout in his dumb old oak tree," Annie said with a superior tone.

"You, young lady, are old enough to know better than to pick at him the way you have been today. Go look in your room. Maybe you left your cell phone here."

Annie scowled at her grandmother. "I used it in the car on our way there, and no, it's not in the car." She turned with her head held high, and strode regally into the house.

Cathy heard the bedroom door shut firmly.

Great. One in a tree, probably crying, and the other shut in her room, plotting revenge. Grandmas are supposed to be fun and spoil kids... I suppose that doesn't hold true when they're living with you.

Cathy pulled rolls out of the freezer and realized she was anticipating the evening with pleasure. They'd never entertained much. Just Janet and whomever she was dating at the time. Henry didn't really have any close friends and as a couple, they'd been out of synch with everyone, having Tina so late in life.

Rob hasn't been back long. Does he socialize with anyone besides Janet?

She started feeling guilty, thinking of Rob as a potential... suitor? *It's a good thing Janet's coming with him.*

She stared out the kitchen window at Henry's chair, remembering him sitting there while Tina set the table for their picnic the Friday before the fourth.

We were so happy. Three weeks ago. And I'm thinking about Rob?

She hugged herself as tears started to flow.

I miss you, Henry. I did love you, really.

She flashed on the moment she said yes to his proposal.

I wasn't expecting that. Was part of me still waiting for Rob? Even then?

She'd avoided Rob those weeks before the wedding. Planning all the details had been her excuse. Henry hadn't seemed to notice. That argument they had at the reception... it had been so clear Rob did love her. But he'd been drunk again.

It made me sad, but Suzie's wrong. I didn't for a minute think about running away with Rob.

She really did love Henry, had loved him even those years his PTSD kept her on edge all the time. She did miss him.

But he's never coming back... And who knows how many years I have left?

Still, her attraction to Rob left her uncomfortable.

Suzie's right. Keep it friends. For now.

The Thin Envelope

Reverend Jones looked at the pile of mail.

Most of it is junk. I'll check emails first.

Long ago, Mrs. Johnson had offered to open and sort mail to save him time, but he had declined, insisting he enjoyed the task. Actually, he knew she had a weakness for gossip and, though he would have liked having the mail filtered, he sometimes got very personal letters from parishioners.

He didn't share his email password for the same reason— not that he expected her to overstep, but to lead her not into temptation.

Today, his email included two personal letters.

The first was from a young man seeking advice on how to tell his parents he was not on a fishing trip, but had eloped and was bringing his bride home tomorrow. The minister wondered if the girl was pregnant or if the impulsiveness was of a purer nature. The parents were going to be very upset if the boy ended up quitting school. The couple was coming to see him first, before going to the parents. He could get more details from them before deciding on his advice.

The second was a newsy report from Mary, a girl from the high school choir, who was spending the summer in Germany with an aunt. Her vitality spilled into the room with her words and photographs. He decided to print and post the letter on the bulletin board out front with all of her pictures, and mention it on Sunday.

Next he dealt with the paper mail. He glanced through the advertisements quickly. The church did not need any new choir robes or hymnals or anything else being offered. That left a few business letters, a bill from the plumber—at least he only charged for parts—and one letter.

As Reverend Jones opened the final envelope, he reflected that he should probably have saved Mary's happy email for last.

This handwriting was unsteady and thin, the writing of a very ill, old, or distraught person. There was only one page. A flat key fell out when he opened it. He began to read.

Dear Reverend Jones,

There are things that happened in 'Nam that I never told Cathy, things that haunt me and make me crazy. Now a dead man's come back and I'm afraid.

If he kills me, please get this key to Cathy.

Tears flooded the Reverend's eyes. He blinked frequently in order to read the details of where Cathy should take the key and the rest of the letter. When he finished, he set it on top of the other mail on his desk and rummaged for a tissue.

Mrs. Johnson came in just then. "Can I help you find something?"

"Yes, do you have any tissues out at your desk?"

"Just a minute."

Ever efficient, Mrs. Johnson returned with a full box.

The minister took one and blew his nose loudly. With another, he wiped his eyes. He'd spoken to the sheriff prior to the funeral. *Henry's death was an accident. They didn't think it was suicide once the mechanic inspected the car. There was no reason to think it was murder...The poor man was paranoid.*

Mrs. Johnson's gaze strayed to the top of the desk, where the letter showed Henry Clark's signature. "A sad letter?"

"That poor Henry Clark," explained the minister, careless in his moment of grief. "We know it was an accident, but I'm afraid he was falling apart."

He suddenly remembered to whom he was speaking and tried to make amends for his indiscretion. "I only tell you this,

Mrs. Johnson, because I know there has been some talk about Cathy—that she is not behaving like a bereaved woman should. I hope you will help stop such rumors, for it is clear from this letter that she had great trials living with Henry. For all they kept a calm surface showing, this letter makes clear the turmoil within her husband, which must have taken its toll on Cathy."

"He was always so steady," insisted the woman.

"This letter was written in confidence, I shouldn't have said anything, but let me assure you, Henry Clark was delusional. I expect you to keep this to yourself, but help stem the gossip about Cathy." The minister paused, wishing he had said nothing. "I know you like to leave early on Mondays to do your errands. Thank you for all your help."

"You're welcome. You know I like to do my part. See you Wednesday."

As the clergyman cleared up a few odds and ends alone, he reflected on Mrs. Johnson's severe gossip habit. If only there was some way to correct it. She did volunteer her time twice a week.

When he started to leave, he noticed the open letter still on his desk. *What if Henry wasn't paranoid? What if he had been right to be afraid? Not likely, but perhaps I should share this with Cathy.*

He didn't want to upset her needlessly, but the key was for her—and he definitely shouldn't leave that lying around. He put the letter and key back in the envelope and took it with him in his pocket. He'd have to decide what to tell her.

There was a youth group fund-raising dinner that night, with a dance afterwards, and that boy and his new wife coming the next day.

I'll take the key to Cathy tomorrow evening or Wednesday.

Making Sure

Well, that's done. Just like last time. So simple, really.

Customers parked on the street out front. The lot was primarily used by people working in the building, so midday it was deserted. And she had backed into her spot, so the car was ready to drive straight out and on down the road, just like Henry. Nothing had been said about his car, so they must not have noticed the loosened bleeding nipple.

Even if they did, it wouldn't matter. They'd never prove it was done on purpose, let alone who had tampered with the brakes.

She'd said she was having dinner at Clark's. She'd probably head straight out there right after work. She'd be late leaving and in a hurry.

Maybe it will happen on the same curve... Pity, she's such a nice girl. But it must be done. She's dangerous.

Rob Comes to Dinner

Rob drove the winding road to Cathy's house. He took the curve on which Henry had died slowly. Edna Johnson was getting her mail out of the box when he drove past. She pursed her lips in disapproval.

I wish Janet was with me. That would look better.

But Janet had called to say she had to work late, that he should go on ahead and fix Tommy's bike before dinner. She'd drive herself.

No one was in sight when he pulled into the yard. He walked up to the house and knocked on the screen door, calling out, "Anybody home?"

"Come on in, Rob. I'm in the kitchen—right through the mudroom."

It hit Rob that he had never been in this house. *My best friend and the girl we both loved had a whole life here that didn't include me.* "Should I take off my shoes?"

"Only when it's been raining." Cathy finished spinning the greens she'd picked for dinner.

Rob entered the kitchen as she rinsed her hands. "This is a nice place."

"We like it. We bought it just before Tina was born... Where's Janet?"

Cathy sounds as awkward as I feel. "She had to work late. Where are the kids?"

Cathy dried her hands and risked a quick smile in Rob's direction. "Annie's in her room and Tommy's watching television. That smells good."

Rob set a paper bag on the counter. "Two loaves of zucchini bread, still warm."

Tommy came to the doorway. "Hey! You're here!"

"Yep. Want to get that bike fixed before dinner?"

"Yeah! It's in the barn." Tommy bounded across the room and grabbed Rob's hand.

"Did you turn off the TV?" asked Cathy.

"Yep." He pulled Rob toward the mudroom. "Come on."

Relaxed by the boy's enthusiasm, Rob flashed a grin at Cathy.

***

Cathy felt herself warmed by Rob's good nature. She watched him walk to the barn with Tommy. She couldn't hear, but she could see they were chatting companionably.

She decided to try talking Annie out of her room, to settle things before dinner. She went and knocked on the door. No answer. "Annie?" She opened it a crack.

The girl was lying face down on the bed, her panda clutched with one arm, her face against it.

"Annie?" Cathy repeated softly.

Annie's eyes opened to slits and she slowly rolled over and stretched, then rubbed her eyes. She sat up, dropped her feet to the floor, and blinked a few times. "What time's it?"

"Quarter after five."

The sleepy eyes flew open. "Are they here already?"

Cathy resisted grinning at her granddaughter's obvious mortification at the prospect of company catching her taking a nap like a little baby.

So much like her mother at that age. "Rob is out in the barn with Tommy, fixing his bike. Janet's going to be late."

Annie yawned, stood up, and stretched some more. Then she paused and looked at her grandmother, remembering their earlier spat. "We stayed up pretty late last night. Sorry I was such a brat."

Cathy leaned forward as if sharing a secret. "We all have our bratty moments."

"I get tired of being dependable and acting grown-up all the time. Mom always expects me to watch Tommy. I have to keep him out of trouble." Her body slumped. "Especially since Dad left."

"Some of that's normal, because you're older, but no one wants you to grow up yet. Being a kid is too important." Cathy walked over and gave Annie a hug.

"We shouldn't have been acting like that while you were driving, though. Sorry."

"Apology accepted. Let's have a nice evening."

Annie smiled. "Okay."

***

Edna Johnson ignored the fact her husband was watching the news on television. She always talked to him anyway. Sometimes he heard, more often he didn't. It was irrelevant to his wife. Though she would often complain that he never listened, she didn't really care for him to respond. She simply wanted to talk. As long as he was in the room, she couldn't be accused of talking to herself, though in reality she was doing that very thing.

"Bold as brass, that's what he is, coming up to see her at the home that poor man made for her, so soon. And at this time of day, too. Right in front of those children! The Reverend Mr. Jones may think Henry Clark was paranoid, but maybe he had good cause for suspicions. Tch. It's a disgrace, that's all there is to it."

Mr. Johnson roused himself slightly to say, "Yes, dear."

His wife looked at him and saw he was totally absorbed in the news. "You never listen to a word I say. If I want an intelligent conversation, I guess I'll have to call Marybelle."

Except it's dinnertime. I'll call after we eat.

Edna nodded, pleased with her decision. People really should be aware of what was going on, especially if the minister was going to brush off Henry's letter.

It was probably just that his wife had been seeing that Rob on the sly, but maybe it wasn't really an accident.

At first Edna was shocked by that thought, then she resolved to take action. If there had been foul play, the minister must not be allowed to cover it up. He was far too lenient anyway.

The first thing would be to bring pressure on the sheriff to investigate the accident more closely.

Public opinion, that's what'll do it.

One or two calls might be put aside as being from a crank, and Edna Johnson didn't want that label.

The way to do it is get people talking so the sheriff has to investigate, to settle the matter. I can call Marybelle after dinner, and June White, too.

By the next night, the whole town would be abuzz.

Then I can call the sheriff. Or maybe I should mention the gossip to Reverend Jones when I go in on Wednesday and let him call the sheriff.

While Mrs. Johnson would like credit for bringing the matter to the authorities, the pastor was the one who had the letter, which would cement the need for a proper investigation.

Yes, that will work.

She went about making dinner, humming.

Edna Johnson was quite pleased with herself.

Another Accident

Janet turned off the computer. *Five-thirty.*

She silently cursed Steve while she went through her office-closing rituals. He'd been able to leave at four-thirty. She'd had to stay late to finish reports. If he'd only apologized for her having to go to his mother's to pick up the folio he had forgotten, it would have helped her mood. But instead, he complained sharply about how long she had been gone. Without that excursion, she could have left at the same time he did. She was only leaving now because she worked straight through lunch. Clattering down the stairs, she moved her thoughts ahead to Cathy's, eager to go straight out there.

But when she got into her car, she realized she had to go home for the potato salad.

Nuts.

The street bordering on the parking lot fed right into the road out to Cathy's. But she'd have to go across town first. She'd planned on that earlier. It was being so late that made the prospect one more irritation in a bad day.

I need to shake this mood. Just as well I have to go get the salad.

She pulled out of her space, drove slowly across the parking lot and into the street.

At least there's no traffic. One good thing about staying in this tiny town.

Approaching a stop sign, she noticed Kevin's Land Rover SUV coming down Chestnut from her right. With no stop on his side, he was about to enter the intersection when she braked, but the pedal went down too easily and her car veered to the right. Realizing she was going to spin into Kevin's path, she blasted the horn. Fortunately, there was a slight uphill slope and she pulled to the side of the road as her car slowed and stopped against the curb.

Having made his own evasive maneuvers to avoid a collision, Kevin came back and pulled in behind her. He ran up and yanked her door open. "What the hell were you doing?"

Still gripping the steering wheel, pale and eyes wide, she turned to look at him silently.

His anger evaporated. "Are you okay? Did your brakes go out?"

She nodded.

"I'll call Tony, tell him where to pick it up, then give you a ride home."

She nodded again. Her mouth worked, trying to talk.

"Come on." Kevin gently helped her out of her car and walked her to his passenger seat.

Janet leaned against him. *I'd forgotten how good his body feels. Strong, lean. Safe.* Before getting in, she managed to speak. "If I didn't have to get the potato salad, I would have been driving out to Cathy's." She started shaking violently.

Kevin wrapped her in his arms and stroked her back. "You're okay. You're okay now. No one got hurt." He kissed the top of her head. "I'm so glad you're okay."

Once she was in the car, he called Tony. "Her brakes went out. She was supposed to drive out to Clarks'. If she had, she'd have wrecked on one of those curves."

Janet heard his voice catch on the last sentence. *He does care.*

Kevin turned on the heater when he got in the car. It wasn't cold, but she was still shivering from shock. When they got to her house, he walked her inside. "I'm not going to leave you home alone." He sat on a stool at the counter.

She smiled weakly. "Thanks." She started to tear up. *I want to be in his arms.*

As if he had heard her thought, he came over and embraced her again. "I don't know what I'd do if anything happened to you."

Yes, that's what I want to hear and this feels so good but...

Janet gently disengaged. "You'd manage. Your sweet young thing would help you through."

Kevin took her hand. "That was a mistake and it's over. I'm sorry I hurt you."

Janet pulled her hand away and hugged herself, searching his face for the truth. *He is sorry.* "We need to talk. Let me put on some warmer clothes. I feel so cold... and I need to call Cathy."

"I can drive you out there, if you still want to go."

He wants to be with me. She looked at the time on her phone and was surprised to realize it wasn't even six.

"Okay. I don't need to call then. The potato salad's in the fridge. You can take it out while I change. I'll be ready in a minute... and we can talk in the car."

Where I won't be confused by being in your arms.

***

Tommy tested the repaired bicycle by riding down the driveway.

"That was trickier than I expected." Rob started putting his tools away.

Cathy smiled as she watched her grandson turn and race back to them. "Thank you, in case he forgot to say so."

"He remembered. He was a good helper, too."

Tommy braked beside them. "It rides great now!"

"Who's that?" asked Annie as the Land Rover started up the driveway. "I think Janet's in the passenger seat."

Cathy peered at the vehicle coming toward them. "That's Kevin's car. Janet used to date him, before you came to stay with us. Tommy, stay up here until they park."

"She was still getting over that when I moved back to town." Rob put his tool kit in his truck. "Said he traded her in for a newer model."

"Her car?" asked Tommy.

Annie rolled her eyes. "You should put your bike away so we can help with dinner."

As Tommy followed Annie's directions, the SUV stopped. Cathy walked forward to the passenger side and opened the door.

Janet handed her the bowl of potato salad and started explaining as she got out. "My brakes failed and I almost T-boned Kevin on Chestnut and Tony is taking it to his garage and I didn't want to call and tell you over the phone. So Kevin gave me a ride home for the salad and offered to drive me out here."

"She was really shaken up," said Kevin.

"You'll stay for dinner?" Cathy asked him in spite of the icy rock in her stomach. *Janet's brakes failed? Like Henry's?*

"I'd love to," he answered.

Cathy handed him the salad bowl. "You remember where the picnic table is?"

"Sure," said Kevin. "Want me to start up the grill?"

Cathy nodded. "I have Angus burgers. You grill them from frozen, so a medium flame." She put her arm around Janet and led her into the house. "Did you report it?"

"No. There was no accident. I didn't hit anything, I pointed the car uphill and coasted off the road."

"But, your brakes..."

"You know my car, Cathy. It really freaked me out, the timing, but the miracle is that this never happened before. That car has 200,000 miles on it and I hadn't checked my brakes or anything else since Kevin and I broke up. I got lazy when he was around to do my car maintenance. It was my own fault, Cath."

"You're sure?"

Janet nodded. "I'm lucky I'd left the salad at home so I was in town and lucky that Kevin's the one I almost hit." Janet grinned happily. "He has been completely protective and caring."

"What about the sweet young thing?"

"History. She landed her dream job in Boston and left two days ago. But he said it was a meaningless fling, that he's always done something stupid like that when he started getting too serious about someone. He apologized for hurting me and said it will never happen again if I give him another chance. "

Evening

Edna Johnson put her cell phone away.

That should do it.

She'd worked the conversations with June and Marybelle carefully. She didn't want them to know her plan. She had to infer and hint that there might have been something wrong with Henry's death, yet make it sound like she didn't believe it. She'd sounded like she agreed with the pastor that Henry Clark had been losing his buttons and that Cathy was the victim. That made June and Marybelle take the offensive, telling her she was pretty naïve if she didn't realize there was something going on between Cathy and Rob, probably before Henry's so-called accident.

By Wednesday, the rumors should be flying full force and I'll be able to convince Reverend Jones to do his duty and take that letter to the sheriff. Then they'll have to investigate.

She only regretted that there was no way she could take credit. She sighed her martyr's sigh.

Ah well, the important thing is to see it's done.

She was but a tool for justice.

***

After dinner, the adults and children sat around the dining room table, playing Michigan Rummy. Janet played the fourth pay card and pulled in all the remaining chips. "Oh, and I have the ace and I am out!" She played her last card with a flourish.

Everyone groaned as they counted how many cards they had left and passed that many chips to her. Rob complained for all of them, "You've been winning every hand."

"True." Janet gloated. Most of the chips were in front of her. "It's been a lucky day for me, but I do have to work tomorrow."

And maybe I'll invite Kevin in when he takes me home. I think I believe him that he really does care.

She pushed her chips to the center and everyone else followed suit. Cathy collected the cards. Tommy stifled a yawn.

"Bedtime," said Annie.

"You're not my boss."

"Am tomorrow. Grandma has a business appointment and if you don't want to be stuck sitting in an office waiting for her, you need to listen to me."

"No fair." Tommy grumbled. "The bad man—"

Janet cut him off. "Come on, Tommy. If you brush your teeth fast, I'll tell you a story before I leave." *No need to end a pleasant evening with a spat between the kids.*

"About Grandpa? When he was a kid?"

"Sure."

Once Tommy was settled in bed and the story was over, Janet gave him a kiss on the forehead. "Good night, buddy."

When she went back downstairs, Kevin had already taken off, leaving Rob to drive her home. She swallowed her disappointment.

Tuesday, July 26, 2022: An Eventful Day

The Reverend

The next morning, Reverend Mr. Jones watched the sunrise while he munched on a piece of toast with strawberry jam. The clouds were beautiful shades of red and pink. He didn't ordinarily get up this early.

I really should—it's a peaceful time of day. He sipped his orange juice. It hadn't been a peaceful night. He hadn't slept well at all. He was being blessed with the sunrise because he had been cursed with insomnia.

That letter from Henry Clark. The letter had hinted at a devastating secret from Henry's past, now come back to haunt him with guilt. Henry had lived in this town all his life. He may have been moody from time to time, but he'd always been well-liked. The fear expressed in that letter rose well into the level of paranoia—unless he really did have reason to be afraid.

What if I'm wrong? Should I give it to the sheriff? But Henry said to give it to Cathy if anything happened to him. I'll call her this morning. Maybe she can allay my doubts.

Considering the early hour, he decided to text: Please call or stop to see me this morning. I have a letter from your husband and a key for a safety deposit box in Winton.

Winton Truck Stop

Kevin sat in a corner booth in the Winton Truck Stop diner, lost in thought. *Janet seemed to believe me last night.*

He'd explained that the stupid meaningless fling was his habitual reaction to a relationship getting too serious. He regretted hurting her and wouldn't let that happen again.

But I've never really felt this way about anyone before. I've got to come out and tell her that I love her, that I want to spend the rest of our lives together.

He'd left Rob to take Janet home the night before to avoid jumping into bed with her. *I'm doing it right this time.*

But he was still nervous about his decision to buy a ring and propose. *She could say no. She's never been married, either.*

He fretted about where to ask her. Not in public. She could say yes out of embarrassment. That would be awful. It has to be special, though. A nice restaurant. A quiet corner where no one will hear.

Don't pull out the ring until after she answers? Or start with it so she knows I'm serious and have thought it through?

His thoughts were interrupted by a commotion across the room.

A large bald man with an ugly scar on his temple slammed his fists on the table and snarled at the waitress, who was taking care of a group of truckers. "How about some service? Or are you paid to stand there talking?"

She started to reply smartly, her hand on her hip, but cut her words off when she looked at the irate customer. She scurried out back to get his order.

Maybe I'll finally get my food, too. Kevin was smiling as his eyes met the angry gaze of the stranger. He felt his face melt into a blank mask automatically. He'd been trained to show no expression in case of capture. His immediate reaction to this man was that he was the enemy, a very dangerous person.

Kevin forced himself to concentrate on his food, which was brought out with the angry customer's meal. Kevin hadn't felt fear like that in a long time. He was glad the man was no one to him and was surprised at the violence of his reaction to a stranger. He told himself to let it go. *He's probably just passing through and I'll never see him again.*

After a peripheral glance assured him the man was just eating his food, Kevin forced his thoughts back to the day ahead of him, and the future beyond. *God, I hope she says yes.*

Annie

Annie yawned as she made her way into the kitchen where her grandmother was wiping her hands on a towel. "Morning, Grandma. Tommy's still asleep."

"Good morning." Cathy went to her purse on the shelf and rummaged in it for her keys.

Annie got a glass out and went to the refrigerator. "When will you be home?"

Keys in hand, Cathy slung her purse over her shoulder. "I have to visit the church before my appointment with Steve Hillman, and I need to drive over to Winton. But I should still be back by noon... Oh, and Suzie called. She found your cell phone. I'll get you a new one."

"Why?" Annie held the juice bottle over her glass without pouring.

"Her gardener brought it to her, said they hit it with the mower this morning. It probably dropped out of your pants when you carried them inside after swimming."

Annie groaned. "All of my contacts..."

"I'm sure they're backed up in the cloud. It was a pre-paid, wasn't it?"

"Yeah."

"Well, I have your number in mine. I'll get it transferred to a new one while I'm in Winton. I think they'll be able to port your contacts to the new phone, too."

"Thank you."

"Meanwhile, I put a list of emergency numbers by the phone near the front door." Cathy waved her hand in that direction.

"Okay." Annie didn't admit she had never used a landline. *It can't be that hard. It's still a phone.*

"Good. It's supposed to storm sometime today. You're sure you're okay with this?" Cathy stopped by the door to the mudroom.

"Sure. I used to babysit for the kids next door sometimes, when they knew Mom was home for back-up."

"Well, Janet was supposed to be the back-up for you today, but her car's in the shop. If you need help, you can call my cell, and if you need someone quickly, Mrs. Johnson's number is on the list, too."

Like I'd ever call Mrs. Johnson. Annie smiled. "Don't worry. If we went with you, I'd be watching Tommy while you do your business stuff anyway and that would be way harder than having him watch TV here."

"Okay. No creek."

"No creek."

Cathy's Morning

The pastor met Cathy at the church and handed her the letter first.

Dear Reverend Jones,

There are things that happened in 'Nam that I never told Cathy, things that haunt me and make me crazy. Now a dead man's come back and I'm afraid. If something happens to me, please get this key to Cathy.

It's for safety deposit box A163 at First National Bank in Winton. There's a letter for her there, and she can decide if she wants to know the rest. She put up with so much when we were first married and it's happening again. I can't sleep. I don't think he'll hurt her, I think he just wants to torture me, but if I'm wrong and we're both dead, give this to the sheriff.

The signature was barely legible as Henry's. Cathy sighed.

"It arrived yesterday," explained Reverend Jones. "You'd mentioned his PTSD to me before, so that was my first thought, that it was back, but the way he died—"

"The sheriff said it was an accident." Cathy blinked back tears. "A dead man after him? He really was losing it."

"Maybe something in the box will explain why he was so fearful."

"I hope so."

"Would you like me to come with you?" he asked, fervently hoping she wouldn't when he had such a busy day ahead.

"No. I think I want to do this by myself." She put the key on her keyring. "Thanks. I'll let you know if it makes sense."

"If you need to talk, I'm here."

Cathy arrived at Steve Hillman's ready to take care of business. She was surprised to see Mrs. Hillman seated in the outer office, drinking a cup of coffee. "Good morning."

"Good morning," the elderly woman replied.

"You're early," said Janet. "We didn't expect you until ten."

"I know, but I was hoping I could get in to see Steve first thing."

"He just got here a few minutes ago and he's on the phone." Janet waved at the landline on her desk, where a button glowed. "I'll check with him as soon as that's done. Coffee?"

Cathy nodded.

Mrs. Hillman looked up. "Stevie gave me a ride up town so I can do some errands this morning. He doesn't like me driving." Her face puckered up in disapproval, then relaxed. "You're early for your appointment?"

Cathy nodded. "I have to go to Winton and I don't want to leave the kids home alone too long. Annie may be old enough to babysit, but Tommy doesn't always listen to her. And the thunderstorms they promised look like they may move in sooner than expected."

Janet poured a cup of coffee for Cathy. "What was Tommy saying about a bad man last night? Before I interrupted him?"

"Oh, some guy bumped into Henry at the fair and Tommy got it into his head that the man was bad, probably because he was big and bald and it was dark out. Tommy said he had black eyes."

"I passed a big bald stranger on the stairs here yesterday. Didn't scare me, but he'd probably be really big to Tommy. Why are you going to Winton?"

"Henry had a safety deposit box at First National. He sent the key to the pastor with a paranoid note saying to give it to the police if something happened to both of us."

Janet checked the landline and pushed the intercom button. "Steve, Cathy's here. Can you see her now?"

"Sure."

Cathy entered the inner office and Mrs. Hillman bid Janet farewell.

***

Once she was outside, Mrs. Hillman pulled out her cell phone and dialed her favorite son. She told him everything she had heard. He didn't seem to take seriously the danger of having been seen by the children and Janet. Or even that Henry had suggested the pastor call the police.

"He didn't call the cops. He gave the key to Cathy, Mother. That's great. It's the only way I could get to it. I'm already in Winton. Whatever evidence Henry had, I'll get it away from her before she talks to anyone."

"What if she calls the police from the bank?"

"Don't worry about it. I'll take care of her."

Dave hung up the phone. An envelope. Whatever Henry had against him fit into an envelope. He could get that away from Cathy easily. *If anyone even cares anymore. I just liked making you squirm, Henry. And the money.*

Growing Storm

Cathy rushed toward the cell phone store to get Annie's phone replaced before going to the bank. She looked up at the dark clouds approaching all too rapidly.

I'll never beat the storm home.

A man coming out of a store bumped right into her, then grabbed her arm to steady her. He apologized profusely.

"Kevin!" She took in the face of the man—and the jewelry store behind him.

"Cathy! I'm so sorry. I wasn't looking where I was going." He apologized again. "Are you okay?"

He sounds like one of the kids when I've just missed catching them getting into something. A jewelry store?

Cathy smiled. "It was nice seeing you again last night."

"It was good to be there, with Janet... I was sorry to hear about Henry." He paused with his mouth partway open, clearly trying to formulate his next words. "Janet and Rob..."

"Have been great. Except Janet's already pushing him at me."

Kevin smiled, clearly relieved. "I kind of thought that's what was going on. So I was right to leave when I did? So he'd take her home?"

"Well, Janet was a little disappointed, I think."

Kevin's smile broadened. "I need to get going." He waved at his car, parked straight across the street. "Thanks."

Cathy looked at the darkening sky.

I wanted to be home by now. Steve didn't have to explain everything in that much detail—but I guess he wanted to make sure I understood.

She gave herself a shake.

Standing on the sidewalk isn't helping.

***

Kevin watched Cathy walk briskly down the street as he got into his car. Then he noticed the man from the diner that morning. He seemed to be following Cathy.

No, the guy has a perfect right to be walking down the same street. I need to remember I'm retired.

***

Rob dropped by Tony's garage late that morning to check on Janet's car. He waited while Tony talked with a customer.

"I'll have to replace this whole section of pipe." Tony pointed toward the belly of the car on the lift. "I don't have time today."

"I can't drive the car like this, but I have appointments all afternoon. I'm a salesman, you know, I can't afford to be without my car. Can't you find the time somehow?"

"I suppose I could work through lunch, but it'll cost you extra."

"Not as much as missing my contacts."

"Okay." Tony turned to Rob. "What do you need?"

"I told Janet I'd stop by to check on her car. Have you had a chance to look at it?"

"Nah, the morning's been crazy, and my afternoon's booked, too. But, since I'm working through lunch anyway, I'll put it up, once I'm done with this guy's exhaust."

"Can I get you something from the deli?"

"No thanks, I've got a sandwich." Tony started pulling out tools.

Rob spoke to his back. "Well, while you fix that car, I'll go get something for myself, and then I'll be back."

"Okay. See you shortly."

***

Kevin pulled into a parking space downtown as the noon whistle blew. He raced toward the building that housed Steve

Hillman's office, hoping to catch Janet for lunch. He'd finally decided to commit; he didn't want to wait. In the hallway he saw her boss about to leave through the back door.

"Steve! Is Janet still up in the office?"

"She was on the phone when I left. I think she brought her lunch today."

"Well, I want to take her out. Could you spare her a least part of the afternoon?"

"Sure. Unless she knows something that has to be done, she can have the rest of the day off."

"Thanks."

Knowing Janet's preference for the stairs, Kevin ran up them to avoid missing her if she was going out after all. He needn't have worried. He found her at her desk, a paper bag in front of her.

"Put that away. I'm taking you to lunch at the Lakeside Inn. Steve said you can have the afternoon off as far as he's concerned."

Janet stared at Kevin. He was untypically disheveled and out of breath.

"The Lakeside?" She constrained conflicting emotions and asked quietly, "So... is that an invitation or an order?"

"I'm sorry. I was afraid I'd miss you. Will you have lunch with me? I have a lot I want to tell you and to talk over with you."

Curiosity won over hurt that he'd left Rob to drive her home the night before. "Okay."

*****

"Swiss on whole wheat with sprouts, to go, please."

"You got it, Rob. You want mustard or mayo?"

"Mustard, please."

Rob watched his sandwich being made. The door chimed and Steve Hillman entered.

Rob raised a hand in greeting. "Hi, Steve. Say, you can tell Janet I'll be over right after lunch to let her know what's wrong with her car."

"Her car?"

"Yeah, didn't she tell you? Her brakes quit on her last night. She almost rammed into someone."

Steve's eyebrows drew together. "No, I was on the phone when she got to work and with clients all morning. No one was hurt?"

"No, but it's lucky she was in town. If she'd gone straight out to Cathy's, she'd probably have wrecked on the same curve where Henry died."

"There you are Rob." The deli clerk passed the wrapped sandwich over the counter. "What can I make for you, Mr. Hillman?"

Steve stared vacantly.

"Mr. Hillman?"

"Oh, um... I've changed my mind... I think I'll go home for lunch, take the rest of the day off." He turned to Rob. "Janet's with Kevin. They were going somewhere for lunch. I don't think she'll go back to the office." Steve drifted out the door.

The Bank

Cathy fretted as she waited in the lunchtime-long line at the bank. *I should have done the banking first. I told Annie I'd be back by now.*

She considered calling to check on the kids, but decided to wait until she was on her way home. *Annie might take offense. She'll think I don't have confidence in her. I'll wait until I can give her a new arrival time.*

When Cathy finally got to the teller, she was informed she needed to speak to one of the bank's officers to get into the safety deposit box.

Disgusted that she had wasted time in line for nothing, Cathy went over to the junior officer who was taking care of business during the lunch hour. The young man seemed insecure and unsure of his ability to handle this responsibility, but he was courteous and, if anything, overly eager to help. Cathy was tired and anxious to start home. The sky was darkening rapidly, with occasional lightning flashes giving an eerie illumination to the day.

"I would like to get into safety deposit box A163. I have the key here." She also had Henry's letter, but hoped she wouldn't need it.

"And your name?"

"Cathy Clark. The box is probably in my husband's name, Henry Clark."

"Let me see, Clark... Your name is on the box too. You must have signed for it."

Cathy searched her memory and came up blank. "When was it opened?"

"Hm... This can't be right. The box was rented forty-three years ago! It shows your husband checked it once a year, probably when he paid the rental fee. But I don't see your signature anywhere but on the opening documents."

Forty-three years ago. Right after we got married.

A vague memory seemed to surface, Henry concerned about a break-in at his apartment, wanting to put his service documents in a safe place. *He had me sign onto the box "just in case" anything ever happened to him. He said something about military insurance.* "I remember, he got it for his personal papers and wanted me to have access."

"This is so irregular. I'm not sure I should let you into the box without your husband present."

"That's not possible. He passed away earlier this month."

The young man looked completely flustered. "I need to check on that. Would you please take a seat?" He scurried off and disappeared through a door to private realms.

Cathy sat at the desk and watched the storm gathering outside. *The kids are going to be freaked out if it hits there before I get home. I should have brought them with me. Maybe I should come back another day.*

She got up and looked for someone she could tell she was leaving. The young man appeared with a more mature woman, obviously his superior. He went off in another direction, but the woman made a beeline for Cathy.

She reached out for Cathy's hand and shook it. "I'm Mrs. Roberts. I'm so sorry for your loss." The woman led her back to the desk and motioned for her to sit.

Cathy complied, but told her, "I really need to get home. If this has to wait for another day…"

"Not at all," said the woman. "Your husband spoke with me not long ago, to make sure you would still have access to the box. He didn't want to bother you with coming back in to sign again. Since the payments had always been made from a joint account, I told him there would be no problem."

"Good. So can we do that now?"

"Yes, but I wanted to let you know your brother-in-law was here earlier, trying to get into the box. I told him that was absolutely against the law, that you were the only one entitled to access. With your husband deceased, the only reason you can get into it is because you're a co-owner. I'm sorry for the inconvenience, having to come here yourself."

Cathy stared at the woman while she tried to wrap her head around the words. "My brother-in-law?"

"Yes, tall man, bald..."

Tommy's bad man. A chill filled Cathy. "What was his name?"

"He just said he was your brother-in-law." Understanding dawned in Mrs. Robert's face. She leaned forward and lowered her voice. "Are you saying he wasn't?"

Cathy choked out the words quietly. "I don't have a brother-in-law."

"Oh, dear." The woman sat up straight. "I'm certainly glad we didn't give him access, though of course we wouldn't, but who on earth could it have been, I wonder?"

"What did he say when you wouldn't let him into the box?" Cathy whispered hoarsely.

"Oh, he said you would probably be along later, he'd wanted to save you the trip... Are you alright? Is there something wrong?"

"No. No, please, just take me to the box. I'll be fine. I just want to get home."

The woman walked her to the safety deposit box area, where the young man had her sign. He went into the vault with her and turned both keys.

"Would you like to take it to a private room?"

Cathy nodded.

What on earth is in this, Henry? Who is that man?

In the privacy of the room, she opened the box and inhaled sharply.

I'd stopped breathing!

She forced herself to breathe in and out.

A business envelope with her name on it was on top. The only other item in the box was a bulky manila envelope. She started to open the one with her name, but a faint rumble reminded her of the approaching storm. *The kids are home alone. They saw that man.*

She stuffed both envelopes in her purse. She needed to get home and check on the kids. The contents of the envelopes could wait.

The rain started while Cathy hurried toward her car. She thought only of her grandchildren and the mysterious bald man who had known she would be coming to the bank.

The man who apparently knows about this envelope and wanted to get it before I did. The man Tommy saw. Henry told Tommy to let him know if he ever saw that man again. She tried calling the children, but the house line was dead.

If I call the sheriff, they'll say it's just the storm. Janet's without a car. Rob? But all of this started right after he got back to town... He can't be involved... Can he?

As she started her car, she thought of her nosy neighbor.

Why didn't I put Johnsons' number into my cell phone?

Once outside Winton, Cathy accelerated rapidly, fear for the children growing within her. She didn't notice the old pickup following her out of town.

Kevin's Proposal

At Kevin's request, they had been seated at a cozy table for two overlooking the lake, away from the few other lunch patrons.

Janet kept her defenses up, her mind racing.

He said he jumped into that fling because we were getting too serious. He said it would never happen again, that he wanted another chance... But he left me to ride home with Rob. Maybe he just said those things because I was shaken up by my accident. Maybe this is goodbye.

Kevin ordered a bottle of wine and they sat in nervous silence, broken by occasional tries at small talk while each examined the menu.

"The seafood platter is usually excellent," he said.

"Yes, it is," she agreed. "The specialty of the day looks interesting, too, though."

"Maybe we should get one of each and share?"

She wouldn't usually eat this much at lunch, but if this was a farewell meal, at least she'd have leftovers for dinner. "Okay."

The waiter poured wine for both of them before taking their order. Once the server had left, Kevin cleared his throat and took a rather large sip of wine, as if for courage.

Janet sat still, waiting.

Maybe he wants to go back to our no-strings relationship. Hell, why not? I'm seventy. It's better than being alone.

"Well, I promised I'd explain before we ate..." Kevin started abruptly, then paused, visibly collecting himself. "I've thought this over carefully. You know I've never been in a serious relationship, one with a future, because... well, I always used the excuse that I didn't know what my future held, but really I never met anyone I wanted to be with all the time, forever."

Janet took a gulp of her wine. "I know. It's simply not who you are. I understood that when we got involved. You didn't pretend our relationship was anything more than casual."

"But I know what I want my future to look like now. A little late in life, but all of my training was for covert operations, distrusting people, taking risks, always aware my cover could be blown at any time..."

"I know. Of course you can't chance being close enough to trust someone."

"But I trust you, Janet. I didn't realize how much until I walked away from you, but I miss that closeness. I want to be with you, Janet. Forever." He pulled the ring box from his pocket and opened it toward her with eyebrows raised in fearful question.

Janet's mouth dropped open when she saw the marquise-cut diamond. She looked at him and smiled.

Seeing the answer on her face, Kevin took the plunge. "I love you, Janet. I want to spend the rest of my life with you. Will you marry me?"

She nodded. "Yes. Yes."

"If you don't like the ring, we can take it back and you can choose another, but I wanted to have one to give you."

"It's perfect." She held out her hand so he could slide it onto her finger. "Oh Kevin, I was so afraid I was going to lose you. I love you."

They leaned across the table to kiss.

The waiter cleared his throat, his eyes looking up. "Excuse me, your entrees."

With embarrassed murmurs, Kevin and Janet drew back into their seats to allow the waiter to serve their meals.

Tony's Discovery

Tony put Janet's car up on the lift to check the brake line. When he saw the bleeding nipple on the driver's front side was open, his throat closed up and he struggled for breath.

It wasn't me. I did tighten down Henry's that morning. Someone's doing this on purpose.

The realization struck him hard.

I should have told the sheriff.

He walked away from the car and sat at his desk, wondering how much trouble he'd be in if he told the whole truth now. He'd said Henry's car had experienced a leak in the brake system.

Maybe I could just tell them about this car.

But Henry's was sitting in the junk yard. They'd take another look at it now.

Better to tell them about both.

He was reaching for the phone when Rob came back from the deli.

Tony looked at Rob, his decision made. "Someone had opened the front bleeding nipple on the driver's side."

"You mean on purpose?" Rob asked in disbelief.

"And Henry's." Tony picked up the phone and dialed the sheriff while he continued explaining. "I worked on his car that morning. I thought it was my mistake. But someone messed with both cars. It can't be a coincidence. Parked in the same lot? But how could some kid pull the same prank after Henry was killed? I don't get it."

"Most of the day that lot is deserted." Rob's mind was spinning. He felt panic rising. *What if Henry was right about someone being a threat to him? But why Janet? And what about Cathy?* "You're sure it couldn't be a freak coincidence?"

Tony shook his head. "No, on Janet's you can see where grit was scraped off when they loosened it." He punched buttons on the phone as he worked his way through menus to get a person at the sheriff's department. *It's not exactly a 911 emergency.*

Janet and Kevin walked into the tiny office, shaking off rain. Janet grinned and greeted everyone cheerfully. "Hi!" She flashed her left hand. When all she got from Rob was a blank stare, she asked, "What's wrong?"

Tony looked up. "Your car was sabotaged—Henry's too."

He waved them out of his office when a person came online at the sheriff's department.

"What is he talking about?" asked Kevin.

Rob explained. "Someone messed with her brakes, Henry's too. Tony worked on Henry's car that morning, so he thought he'd made a mistake somehow."

Janet shivered. "Henry was afraid. What if he wasn't paranoid? What if someone wanted him dead? But why? And why me?"

Kevin pulled her close.

Home Alone

Tommy and Annie sat at the kitchen table in dim daylight.

"When's the power going to go back on?" whined Tommy.

"I don't know."

It had been out for an hour, terminating Tommy's Minecraft game and eliminating the possibility of movies or TV.

"All you've been doing ever since lunch is looking at that dumb old yearbook," Tommy complained. "Come on, play checkers or something with me, will ya?"

"Didn't Grandpa show you how to play solitaire?"

"That's boring. Maybe I could go outside. The rain's almost stopped."

"No. Everything will be wet and Grandma won't want us getting soaked and making a mess coming back inside." Annie used her most adult tone. "She should be home soon."

"Okay, but will you play checkers with me pul-eeze?"

"Fine." Annie capitulated. "But you go get the board. It's in your room, isn't it?"

"Yep. I'll get it right away." Tommy ran for it before she changed her mind.

Annie moved to the dining room table, taking the yearbook with her. She was gazing at the picture of the Three Musketeers when Tommy raced in, his eyes wide.

"Annie," he whispered urgently. "He's out by the garage."

"Who?"

"The bald man. Grandpa told me he was bad."

"What are you talking about?"

"Really, Annie. I saw him. Looking around like he was making sure no one was here."

Annie crossed her arms. "You're making this up just to scare me, aren't you, because I made fun of you when you wigged out this morning, when you woke up and realized Grandma had left us home alone?"

"No. For real. I saw him, out near the garage."

Annie thought about it. Even if Tommy was being silly about the man at the fair, if someone was poking around outside, that wasn't good. She went to the window.

"No, don't let him see you!" cried Tommy.

She moved behind the curtain and peered around the edge, starting to feel a bit uneasy. She heard a click and turned her head. Tommy had locked the deadbolt on the front door and was headed for the kitchen.

What if there really is someone out there? I don't have my cell phone. She glanced across the room at the landline. It had buttons like a cell phone, and she'd answered it once when Grandma's hands were covered in flour. The list of numbers was there, and she could use it for 911.

It'll work. If there's really someone out there. But Tommy's probably trying to scare me, is all.

One More Accident

"Lousy weather out there," proclaimed the sheriff, shaking water off his coat and stomping his feet as he entered the garage where everyone had gathered by the office. "I was on my way over here when your call came in, Tony. Have some more business for you. Cathy Clark this time. I was lucky to spot her car while I was cruising. It was down in a gully."

"Is she alright?" Rob's demand was louder than all the other exclamations.

"I'm not sure how bad she is. The emergency crew took her to the hospital in Winton. She was semi-conscious, not making any sense. Took quite a crack on her head, looked like. May have a broken arm, too. They splinted her up pretty good, to make sure no more damage was done in transport. Looked like someone sideswiped her and kept on driving."

"I'm going to the hospital," announced Rob. "What about the kids? Are they okay?"

"She was alone in the car."

"She mentioned leaving them at home when she came by the office this morning," said Janet. "Kevin and I can go get them and bring them to the hospital."

Rob left hastily.

"How old are these children?" asked the sheriff.

"Annie's a very responsible thirteen," Janet assured him. "Completely capable of watching her nine-year-old brother a few hours. But with Henry's death and Tommy's being afraid of the bald man, I'm sure it's best they see their grandmother as soon as possible."

"What bald man?" demanded Kevin.

The sheriff nodded in agreement. "Mrs. Clark kept muttering something about a bald man and an envelope."

Janet explained. "Tommy saw a big bald man bump into Henry at the carnival and got fixated on him, calls him the bad man, and apparently Henry humored him by saying to let him know if he ever saw the man again."

Kevin groaned. "I saw him. This morning. Following Cathy. I told myself I was imagining things."

"What makes you think it was the same man?" asked the sheriff.

"I'd seen him earlier at a café. He got angry at a waitress for being slow. I worked special ops a long time, Sheriff. I knew he was dangerous. Someone you'd never want to cross alone in a dark alley."

"I saw a tall bald man yesterday," mused Janet. "He was big, but I didn't feel like he was threatening or anything. Of course, I was in a hurry to leave the office and didn't really look at him."

"If he didn't want to be seen? That could be why your brakes were tampered with," said Kevin.

"You're the one Tony called about?" The sheriff looked from Janet to Tony.

"And Henry Clark," Tony reminded him.

Janet blanched. "The children saw him. Can you call the house, Tony?"

"Sure."

Janet rattled off the number and he dialed.

"Not in service," he said. "Storm may have knocked it out."

"You two follow me," commanded the sheriff. "If everything's alright, they'll need you to take them to their grandmother."

The Kids & the Bad Man

Tommy had locked all the windows and doors. If he was pretending to be afraid, he was doing a good job of it. But Annie hadn't seen anything yet. She still peered from behind the curtain at the garage. She was about to give up and chew out Tommy for scaring her when she saw the man slip out of the building. He carried a can.

"He's coming toward the house," she whispered.

Tommy stole a look past her. "That's the gas for the mower!"

Annie took a deep breath, then let it out. She gave Tommy orders in a quiet, firm voice. "Go to the other side of the house and open that window near the TV. Quietly. I'll phone for help."

Tommy rushed off to the window while Annie tried the landline.

Isn't there supposed to be a kind of buzzy noise before I dial? She pushed buttons anyway. 911. Silence. Her stomach sunk. *It's not working.*

She headed for the TV room.

Tommy had the window open. There was a short drop, but their fall would be broken by the bushes.

"Tommy, I think he's going to burn the house down. We have to go out this window and then run for the woods and hope he stays on the other side of the house until we're out of sight. There's no way he knows we're here."

Tommy looked frightened, but tried to take on the role of protector. "Women first."

"Okay, hang like I do and drop. I'll try to catch you."

Annie crawled over the windowsill, legs out first, then let herself down until her arms were fully extended. She was just inches from the bush. She leaned back and fell, landing with her feet in the air, perched in the shrub like some awkward bird. Any other time, Tommy would have been helpless with laughter. Now he followed her through the window silently. As he dropped, they both heard the sound of breaking glass.

"Come on," hissed Annie. She tugged Tommy to his feet. "Run!"

As they entered the woods, the sound of a siren reached them. Annie pulled Tommy behind some brush and they crouched, panting. The sheriff's car pulled into the driveway.

"Who's that behind him?" asked Annie.

"That's the car that guy was driving when he brought Janet for dinner."

Both vehicles disappeared on the other side of the house. The children heard the sheriff shout something, followed by the crack of two shots. Then they heard Janet screaming for them.

"Think it's okay?" asked Tommy.

Annie nodded. "Come on."

The children walked, shaking, hand in hand, across the field.

***

Kevin entered the house first, through the mudroom where the can of gasoline sat unspilled. Janet was shouting up the stairs for the children when he spotted them through the open window by the television.

"Janet, it's okay," he called. "They're okay. They're on their way in." He stuck his head out the window. "Hurry up, kids. You're alright?"

"We're okay!" They both yelled as they ran to the house.

Janet and Kevin met them in the yard and walked them inside to the dining room, where they could sit down. After clarifying they were fine and that there had only been one man, Kevin went outside to watch for the sheriff's return.

"Did the sheriff shoot the bad man?" asked Tommy.

"I don't think so." Janet stood between the children, rubbing their shoulders. "Are you sure you're okay?"

Annie nodded. "I thought Tommy was trying to scare me at first, saying he saw the man Grandpa was afraid of, but then I saw him, too, and he had the gas can."

"And Annie said we should go out the window and hide in the woods!"

"How'd the sheriff know to come?" Annie looked puzzled. "I didn't think the phone was working—and you wouldn't have gotten here that fast, anyway."

Janet took a breath and paused.

Annie interrupted. "Is Grandma alright? She was supposed to be home by now."

"She should be okay. She was in an accident and hit her head pretty hard, so they took her to the hospital. Rob's on his way there and Kevin and I came to get you."

"But why was the sheriff with you?" demanded Tommy. "The bald man made Grandma have her accident, didn't he."

"We don't know for sure. Maybe." Janet took a good look at the children. "You're both soaked from the bushes, so go change quick. You have leaves in your hair, Annie. I'll wait here and when you're ready, we'll take you to the hospital to see your grandma. And throw some clothes into your backpacks, and your toothbrushes. You might stay with me a couple days."

The children scurried to their rooms, anxious to get going. Janet sank into a chair, suddenly drained. She put her head back and closed her eyes, trying to relax. A footstep in the kitchen jolted her back to alertness, her heart racing and her breathing tight and shallow.

"The sheriff's back." Kevin said as he walked into the room.

Janet exhaled loudly and leaned on the table, cupping her face in her hands.

"Janet, are you okay? Where are the kids?"

"Getting changed. You startled me. I wasn't sure it was you."

"I didn't think." He put his arm around her. "I didn't mean to scare you."

"That's okay. I told the kids about Cathy, and that we'd go as soon as they got into dry clothes. They're soaked from the bushes. Did the sheriff catch him?"

"No. He had a pickup parked on a logging road up in the woods. Sheriff got a partial. He's radioing it in." Kevin heaved a sigh. "It was the guy I saw tailing Cathy this morning. Of all the times to stop paying attention to my instincts... I hope she's okay."

Janet took his hand. "It's not your fault."

"It won't be safe for them until he's caught."

"I told the kids they're staying with me for now. Not exactly what I had in mind for tonight, but..." She looked at the diamond on her finger, shrugged and smiled.

"I'll feel better if I stay with you too."

"Good." Janet leaned into him.

The children hurried into the room with their packs.

Tommy was carrying the checkerboard, too, folded up with the pieces inside. "Annie said I should bring this in case we're at the hospital a long time."

"It took hours when Daddy hurt his hand," Annie explained.

"Good idea."

"Thanks. I can bring Grandpa's yearbook, too. Where is it? I left it on the table."

Tommy swiveled his head around, then pointed to the corner, where the book was face down, half open, on the floor.

"How'd it get there?" Annie retrieved it. "Nuts, some of the pages got bent. That man must have thrown it over here, but why would he?"

"Maybe he was startled by the siren, and knocked it off the table by accident," Tommy said.

Annie flattened the pages of the yearbook and slid it into her pack. "Are you sure Grandma's okay?"

Janet clenched her teeth a moment before deciding on the truth. "All I know for sure is she hit her head hard and they took her to the hospital."

"Is anyone there to protect her from the bad man?" Tommy looked ready to fight.

Kevin put a hand on the little boy's shoulder. "Rob's on his way."

"And I have a deputy there already," said the sheriff. He'd come in while they were talking. He noticed the backpacks. "Kids staying with you tonight?"

He was looking at Kevin, assuming they were a couple.

"Yes, they're staying with us until you catch that man." Kevin smiled at Janet.

"Good. He won't get far in that truck, but this is a crime scene. Probably shouldn't have let you back into the house at all, but don't worry about it. If we're lucky, the techs will get some fingerprints off that broken glass or the gas can. Doubt they'll find anything else. Once they get out here and tell me it's okay, I'll lock up if you have a spare key somewhere?"

"It's on a yellow springy thing in the drawer by the refrigerator," said Annie. "It's for the doors and I think Grandpa put a key for the deadbolts on it, too."

"I'll drop it off later at the hospital, when I come talk to Mrs. Clark."

"Can we go now?" Tommy slung his pack over his shoulder. "I want to see Grandma."

"Absolutely," said the sheriff.

He watched them leave from the window, then went into the kitchen. He was pulling the spare key out of the drawer when the landline rang.

Must have been the storm knocked it out.

He answered, "Clark residence.... Oh, hello Reverend. This is Bob Smith, with the sheriff's department. Mrs. Clark was in an accident, they've got her over to the Winton hospital. Janet Delaney and her fella are taking the kids over there... No, wouldn't do any good to come out here tonight. Seems some fellow's after the whole family. Henry's death may not have been an accident after all."

A wave of guilt hit Reverend Jones on the other end of the call. "I should have gone with her." He explained the brief, cryptic letter and the key. "She went to get whatever was in that box."

"You take that letter straight to our headquarters at the county jail in Winton. It's on your way to the hospital."

And I'll get my guys back at the scene looking for that envelope she was muttering about... though most likely the bald man got it. But why would he come to the house, looking to burn it down?

Discovery

Janet strode into the emergency room with the children in tow while Kevin parked the car. She spotted Rob at the information desk. "Rob!"

He turned. "Hi, I was just leaving a message for you to meet me in the waiting room upstairs. They're setting her arm now. There was apparently no skull fracture, but they'll keep her overnight for observation. The sheriff's deputy is with her."

"She's going to be okay, right?" Annie hitched her backpack up higher on her shoulder.

Rob nodded and smiled. "Yes, she should be fine. Her arm is broken, but it's a simple fracture, and she had to have a few stitches right up here by the hairline, where she hit her head, but she came to on the way to the hospital and the doctors don't expect any complications."

"So she can come home?" Annie asked.

Rob shook his head. "They keep anyone who's hit their head that hard overnight, in case they feel sick later. But she's talking now and making sense and she's anxious to see you kids. The sheriff's man told us what happened at the house."

"So when can we see her?" Annie was standing her tallest, trying to look adult.

"They'll take her up to her room once they finish with her arm, then you should be able to see her for a few minutes, Annie. But not for long, because she needs her rest."

"How long?" whispered Tommy, subdued by the hospital atmosphere.

"Just a few minutes."

"No, how long do we have to wait?"

"Oh, the nurse said it would be a half hour or more. She'll come get us."

Kevin caught up to them at the elevator.

"There's a waiting room upstairs," Janet explained. "Good thing you thought to have Tommy bring the checkers, Annie."

"I'd rather look at the yearbook. Someone else play with him."

"Okay," said Rob. "I'll challenge you to a game, Tommy."

"I'm not real good yet."

"That's okay. I haven't played in a long time, so we may be even."

Unlike the emergency room, the waiting room on the second floor was empty when they arrived. Rob and Tommy sat on opposite sides of a small table while Janet and Annie curled up on a couch with the yearbook. Kevin settled into a chair with a magazine, half-watching the checker game.

"This is my teacher," said Annie, pointing at a picture in the yearbook. "She looks the same, her hair's not even that different. A little, maybe. But is this the Mr. Joblanski who owns the hardware store?"

"Sure is." Janet chuckled. "It doesn't look like him at all, does it?"

"No way. I figured it must be some other Joblanski. He had a lot of hair and now he's completely bald. How come that happens to some men and not others?"

"I guess it's hereditary. It does make a difference in the way they look, doesn't it."

"Yep. Here's Grandma with Rob, before she married Grandpa, and here's Grandpa and Rob with their other friend."

"Dave." Janet put a hand on the page. *Innocent times.*

"I'm sure glad Grandpa and Rob didn't go bald. Look how ugly they'd be." Annie covered the tops of the Three Musketeers' heads.

Janet stared, the color draining from her face.

Annie started to say something, but seeing Janet's expression, she looked back at the page where her hand was still in place. "It's him, isn't it!"

"It can't be," denied Janet. "Kevin, Tommy, come here!"

Kevin dropped his magazine and rushed to Janet. "What's the matter?"

Rob and Tommy caught up.

Tommy saw the photo, with Annie's hand still covering the tops of heads. "It's him!"

Janet looked up at Kevin. "You got a good look. Is it?"

Kevin examined the photo before he nodded. "Definitely. He's filled out of course, harder expression, but definitely the same guy."

"That's impossible," said Rob. "Dave died in Vietnam. Henry saw him blown to bits, brought back his dog tags."

Kevin pointed at photo. "The nose and cheekbones, the placement and shape of the eyes—those all stayed the same. And that little scar on his right temple—now he doesn't have hair, you can see it's a lot longer than it looks here."

"About four inches. From a bike accident when we were twelve." Rob looked stunned. "I thought it was Dave's death that messed up Henry so bad."

"More likely, this guy went AWOL and either handed Henry his dog tags or threw them on the ground and Henry picked them up."

Janet took the book from Annie and closed it. "That's why Henry went back for a second tour, Rob, to find him. He is alive. I wasn't paying attention the other day, and it never occurred to me that he was alive, but I saw the scar."

Rob rubbed a hand through his hair. "Henry said he was the only one who made it back from that patrol. You're right, Kevin, Dave probably went AWOL."

"But Dave wouldn't hurt Cathy or Henry or the kids," protested Janet. "Or me."

"Not the Dave you knew." Kevin thought of his own life, how covert ops had demanded he be a different person than he was now. "You don't know what's happened since then. A lot of years have passed. He may have changed more than you could imagine."

"Steve!" Rob snapped his fingers. He turned to Kevin. "He's Dave's brother. I ran into Steve at the deli, told him about Janet's brakes. He acted really strange, walked away without getting any lunch, as if he was in another world."

"Steve probably knows where his brother is," said Janet. She thought of the book on car repairs she'd knocked to the floor. "We need to tell the sheriff."

"Excuse me," interrupted a nurse. "Mrs. Clark is in her room now. You can see her for a few minutes if you like. She's been asking about the children. Just be careful not to tire her out. Keep it short."

"I'll stay here and call the sheriff," said Kevin.

***

Cathy had the head of the bed tilted up when they entered her room. The children rushed to her side, but seeing her head bandaged and her arm in a cast, even Tommy had the sense not to pounce on her.

Cathy smiled. "I'm so glad to see you're okay. The sheriff sent over a guard, and he told me what happened at the house. The doctor was so mad at him, even though he said you were okay. Then finally, the nurse came in while they were putting the cast on my arm and she said you were here and looked fine—I was so scared for you."

Tommy puffed up to brag. "That man did come to the house, but I saw him and told Annie. Then we went out the TV room window and ran and hid in the woods, and Janet and Kevin and the sheriff got there and scared him away."

Janet stood by the door, wondering if she should say anything about Dave Hillman.

Annie held the bed rail. "Does your head hurt much?"

"Yeah, but it'll be okay."

Tommy chimed in. "We figured out who he is, Grandma."

"What? You recognized him?" Cathy searched all their faces.

Janet took a step closer. "It sounds crazy, but we're pretty sure it's Dave Hillman."

"But he's dead. That's why Henry…"

Annie interrupted. "It's him, Grandma. I covered the tops of their heads in the yearbook."

At Cathy's skeptic look, Janet told her the rest, with everyone else nodding.

"Dave…" Cathy looked at each of them, ending with Janet. "He must have run me off the road for that envelope. Henry's secrets. Did they catch him?"

"Not yet, but the kids are staying with us. And if they don't catch Dave before you're out of here, you can stay with us, too."

"Us?"

Janet held up the hand with her new engagement ring. "It's been an eventful day."

Cathy smiled. "Congratulations."

The nurse poked her head into the room. "Best to wrap it up folks."

"Ask that sheriff's deputy to come in, please." Cathy turned to Janet. "He tried to get the envelope from the bank, before I got there. They must have cameras. A current photo may help catch him."

"Good," said Janet. "And Steve may know how to find his brother. I can't believe he had anything to do with the rest."

"Dave... It seems strange to even say his name out loud. He probably destroyed whatever was in that envelope." Cathy grimaced. "The one with my name on it was gone, too. I wish I'd at least read that at the bank."

Evening

"Marybelle? You won't believe what's been going on here today." Edna Johnson's excitement bounced through the connection. "The sheriff's out at the Clark place, and I swear I heard shots fired. Then I saw the children leave with Janet Rodriguez and that boyfriend of hers. The sheriff stayed until more police came." She could tell Marybelle was soaking up every word. "It's obviously a crime scene. I thought the children left with their grandmother this morning, but they must have come back while I was in the shower. Those poor children, having to cope with more tragedy—of course, if their mother wasn't off globe-trotting—not even coming back for her father's funeral..."

***

Once he'd passed Janet and the children to Kevin's protection, Rob slipped back to Cathy's room and sat in the chair beside her bed. He sandwiched her free hand between his and sat there quietly, their shared gaze saying volumes.

Cathy blinked. Tears started to slide down her face. She gently pulled her hand from Rob to wipe them away. "Thank you for being here."

He got a tissue, dabbed her cheeks, then took her hand again. "I was terrified when I heard you were found unconscious. I'm not going to rush you, but Cathy, I never stopped loving you. When I told you to date other people, I knew whatever happened, I could end up dead. I was already thinking that, if Henry was going to be drafted, he wasn't going alone. Then Kent State made me realize I could end up dead staying here, too. I knew I'd be protesting the war if I stayed home."

She smiled. "I was a terrible girlfriend for you. I liked living with blinders on, blocking out anything unpleasant in the world. I never understood how important it was to you to be involved, to fight for things bigger than yourself. I was really proud when you decided to be a medic, though."

"Sometime during basic training, it hit me that the decision I'd made for friendship was leading me into a war I didn't believe in and that I'd have to kill. Being a medic was the only choice I could live with."

"I never stopped loving you, either. Even when you were so angry and self-destructive and I couldn't bear to be with you, I still loved you. I loved Henry, too, though. I still do."

Rob smiled gently. "I've heard it's possible to love more than one person at the same time. And you were right. He was far better husband material than I was back then. That's how I made it through your wedding... I couldn't stay, though."

"It wasn't your political differences with Henry?" Cathy tilted her head a bit.

"No. He always talked like a hawk, but it never felt like he meant it. It always seemed like he was holding something back... Now we know he was." Rob stared out the window.

"If only I'd stayed at the bank and looked through that envelope." Cathy huffed, annoyed with herself. "I didn't even open the one with my name on it. I was so worried about the storm and the kids being home alone. I'll never know what he wrote to me."

Rob returned his gaze to hers and reassured her with a smile. "If they get a good image from the bank, they should find Dave. Maybe he'll still have the letter."

"I can't believe he's alive, that Henry kept that a secret from me all these years." A yawn broke through her words.

He stroked her cheek. "Close your eyes. The kids are safe and I'm not going anywhere. Rest."

She yawned even wider and let her eyelids slide down.

Still holding her hand, Rob leaned forward and kissed her forehead gently, then settled into the chair to watch over her.

***

Janet lived in the home where she'd grown up, a three-bedroom ranch-style fifties house. The basement still had the requisite rec room with its own television set and faux-leather couch. It was a challenge to land on one movie both kids wanted to watch, but once they were ensconced with pizza, popcorn, and non-caffeinated sodas at opposite ends of the sofa, Janet and Kevin went back upstairs to the living room.

"That's a terrible dinner." Janet collapsed in a recliner, exhausted.

"They're practicing for college." Kevin stretched out on the couch.

Janet looked at his straight face and cracked a smile. "You never wanted kids?"

"My lifestyle wasn't right for it. Now I'm too old."

"Not if you'd stuck with that sweet young thing."

"Don't go back to that, please. If you had kids, I'd still want to marry you. But I'm fine borrowing other people's children from time to time. I have a brother who had six of them and they've all created their own broods, and I think the next generation's already on the way. That's plenty of opportunity for enjoying them without the daily responsibility." He wanted to ask whether she'd ever wanted children, but was worried it might be a sore spot. Instead he asked, "Are the kids with Cathy for the whole summer?"

Janet nodded. "Their parents divorced and Tina—you met her last summer, when they came out for the Fourth—she got a great job opportunity, but has to do eight weeks of training abroad... Cathy and Henry were so happy to have the kids for the summer."

"What about their father?"

"Idiot moved on, started a new family to abandon in a few years."

Janet rolled her head, stretching her neck. "In my twenties and thirties, even my forties, I wanted to settle down with the father of my children. I just never found him. And eventually I realized that wasn't going to happen. It's easier now most of my friends are grandparents instead of parents."

"That's how I feel with my brother, like we're closer to the same life now... If you come over here, I'll rub your neck." He dropped his feet, making space for her on the couch.

"I'll take you up on that offer."

Janet went over to the couch and sat with her back to him. After a few minutes, during which the only sounds were an occasional moan of pleasure from Janet and the low noise of the kids' movie downstairs, Kevin sighed. "I'm so glad Cathy's going to be okay. I should have followed him when I thought he was up to no good."

Janet leaned her head to gently squeeze his hand against her shoulder. "We're not supposed to be having that kind of problem. I wish she'd looked inside the envelope, though. I mean, sure, we've figured out it's probably Dave Hillman and that he went AWOL, but there's got to be more to explain how he could do all this. He was always the timid one. I was amazed that he actually enlisted with them."

Kevin kissed the back of her neck. "War changes everyone it touches."

Steve poured more liquor over what was left of his ice. He stared at the once-full bottle, now nearly empty.

Strange, I usually hate scotch.

He wasn't sure whether or not he'd spoken aloud. After hearing about Janet's car, he'd come back to the office from the deli and started drinking. His Beretta was on the desk in case his brother showed up.

When the deputies came, he knew he shouldn't talk to them, but he needed to stop this insanity. He did put his gun back into the desk drawer when they announced themselves from the front office. But when they described the man they were looking for and said they had reason to believe it might be his brother, the floodgates opened. He ignored their note-taking.

"I thought he was dead. They never told me. Henry Clark and my mother. They kept the secret. For decades. Then after Henry died, Dave showed up here and demanded money. Said everything I've ever done with my life, every penny I've made, was rightfully his because his death benefit paid for my degrees."

He gestured grandly at the framed documents on his wall. "I didn't know. I worked. I would have worked more if that's what it took. I wouldn't have taken it if I'd known."

The empty bottle and Steve's demeanor made it clear he was drunk. The officer in charge chose his words carefully. "We're here about your brother, sir. We don't really care about what happened back then."

"I know." Steve cut him off with a wave of his hand. "He started blackmailing Henry Clark first—that's when Henry told me the whole story. He thought I knew Dave was alive, wanted me to convince him to stop. We couldn't turn Dave in to the authorities, 'cause Henry had helped him fake his death and I..." He gestured at his credentials again. "Henry signed up for a second tour, went back to find Dave and turns out my saintly brother was deep in the drug trade and didn't want to be saved... Henry had finally put it all behind him, then Dave showed up, demanding money."

"Where can we find him, sir?"

Steve leaned back and nearly tipped over the chair before he caught himself and leaned forward. "That is the question. You know he is one bad dude, right? I felt guilty about Henry Clark. Figured he drove into that tree on purpose, that Dave drove him to that. Then today I find out Janet's brakes were tampered with, and I know it's because she passed Dave on the stairs. I don't think she even recognized him. She would have been asking questions if she had. Janet is not a shy woman. She is very assertive. Good person to have in my front office..."

"So where can we find him?"

"Have you tried the house? I told them he shouldn't stay in town, but they don't listen to me. Last couple nights he parked his truck in the garage and slept in his old room. I didn't sleep. But if he knows you're on to him, he may be long gone already."

"Who owns the house?"

"It's in my name," he slurred. "She wouldn't move. Didn't have enough income to take care of it. So I bought it. Years ago. She lives there rent free while I pay the mortgage and all the bills... But I can't do anything right, far as she's concerned. Her Davey, now, he's always been a saint."

"Would you mind giving us permission to search the premises? Save us having to get a warrant."

"Absolutely."

"You'll have to come with us."

"If you'll bring me back here once you're in. I do not want to deal with my mother's outrage."

"Can do." The officer who'd done most of the questioning steadied Steve's arm as he got up from his chair. *We're certainly not letting you drive anywhere.* Besides, it was better if no one realized how drunk Steve was when he gave them permission to search his house for his brother. It could create problems with any evidence they collected if he changed his mind later.

***

Mrs. Hillman greeted the sheriff and his officers at the door in her slippers and a housecoat. "I'm sorry, this is my son's house. I can't really give you permission to come in here and make who-knows-what kind of mess. I've seen those cop shows where they wreck a place claiming they're searching it."

"Your son has given us his permission." The sheriff pointed to the car where Steve gave a wave indicating the deputies were allowed to enter.

Reluctantly, slowly, Mrs. Hillman stepped aside. "Be considerate. Don't leave it looking like a tornado went through. What do you want, anyway? What has Stevie done?"

"He's done nothing, Mrs. Hillman. However, we have reason to believe your other son is alive and perpetrating crimes."

"Nonsense. Davey died in Vietnam." She turned away and hid her face in a tissue.

The only things they were looking for were the man himself and the mysterious large envelope. After a thorough search the sheriff offered his apologies and they left. The car with Stevie in it had already returned him to his office, as promised.

"Hmph. Ingrate." Mrs. Hillman walked to the top of the attic stairs and spoke quietly to the empty room. "Best stay put for now. I'm pretty sure they left one fella to watch the house. No telling what newfangled electronic gear they have."

Then she went downstairs, got her keys, locked up, and drove to Steve's office.

***

Steve had stopped drinking. They hadn't found Dave. He sat facing the door with his Beretta in his lap. When at last he heard the outer office door open and close, he wiped his icy palms across the legs of his pants. He gripped the handgun properly, eased off the safety, and pointed it at the door.

Slowly, breathe slow and easy. Squeeze at the bottom of the exhale. He was a good shot at the pistol range. He raised the weapon, ready to fire. The knob turned and the door swung open all in one motion.

"What are you doing?" demanded his mother, her voice angry rather than afraid.

"I thought you were Dave." He dropped the weapon to his lap and slid the safety into place.

Would I have been able to pull the trigger if it was Dave? He was decent to me when we were kids. It was after he died she turned him into a saint... He scares the hell out of me now. He's not the brother who enlisted to stand by his buddy, even though he was scared shitless.

His mother came across the room and leaned on his desk, shoving her face at him. "What kind of reception would that be for your brother? What's wrong with you?"

"He killed Henry, Mother, and tried to kill Janet, and Cathy, even the children. He was going to burn the house down with them in it."

His mother scoffed. "Who told you that? The sheriff? They don't know what they're talking about."

"Too many people have seen him. I told him he should stay away."

"Fine brother you are." She curled her lip in disgust. "After all he's been through."

There's no point. She'll never believe what he's done. "Is he gone? They didn't find him."

"No. He's hiding in that little space off the attic you used to hide in when you were little. They missed it. Since you've co-operated with the sheriff, they'll never suspect you. You'll drive him out of here."

"You haven't been listening to me. He's a murderer!"

"I heard you," she said sharply. "Your brother called me. He had to get rid of his truck, the sheriff was after him. I picked him up and got him home before you turned into a Judas."

"You can't help him. He killed Henry Clark. He's insane!" Steve pleaded.

"What do you know about insane," she snapped. She hit her fists on his desk. "Insane is the kind of world he found himself in, in the name of duty to his country. War is the murderer. It killed my boy. Now he's here. Of course I can help him. I can do anything I have to, to protect him. You wouldn't understand that. You've always had it soft. You owe your brother, Steven." She pointed and shook her hand at him. "Don't you forget that!"

"I never asked for that kind of help. I could have put myself through school, and I would have if I'd known."

"Yes, you would have. That's why I never told you. We got that insurance money legitimately. Davey did die, in a very real sense. What kind of life could he lead, always on the run? And for what? For running away from that hell? I know what war is. I know what soldiers are led into doing. Don't you act holier-than-thou with me or your brother." Her tone switched from outrage to wheedling. "Come with me now. You need to drive him away from here tomorrow. We'll stop and let them check my car before we park in the garage. They won't see him get into it, and they won't bother checking it when you leave because they already searched the house with your permission. You'll wait until morning, same as a regular day."

Steve slipped the gun into his jacket pocket, then pretended to put it away in a side drawer before he got up to leave with her.

I could refuse and call the sheriff's office right now, tell them where to find him. But she'll never forgive me. There's time. Maybe I can talk some sense into her. But I'm not going to be in that house with him unarmed.

Wednesday, July 27, 2022: Endings

Morning

Rob poured himself a cup of coffee while the sky began to lighten. They'd made him go home at the end of visiting hours the night before. He rumpled his hair roughly and stretched to finish waking up.

I can probably slip in early. They said the doctor will come by on morning rounds and release her, most likely. Not this early, though.

He went downstairs to collect mail from the day before. It was piled up below a slot in the front door of the studio. There were several large envelopes—portfolios from artists and photographers who wanted to display on the side he was opening to others—and advertisements. He tossed out the ads and opened the first portfolio while he headed back upstairs for his coffee.

I should eat something, too.

He set the mail aside while he ate and washed up. He was eager to get back to Cathy, but he didn't want to spend his time with her viewing portfolios, so he decided to finish looking through the mail before going to the hospital. He left the bulky one with no return address for last.

***

Annie woke up on the couch in the basement, a blanket over her, her feet overlapping Tommy's. He had his own blanket. It took a moment to realize they were in Janet's rec room. Annie slipped off the couch and tiptoed up the stairs. Janet and Kevin were in the kitchen making breakfast while they drank coffee.

Kevin was scrambling eggs. "Figured we could all use a good meal to start the day."

Janet was pouring orange juice.

"Can I get a shower?" Annie yawned. "I feel totally gross and my face is greasy."

"The eggs are almost done. Why don't you eat first?"

"Okay." She sat down and emptied a glass of juice.

"More?" Janet filled the glass again when Annie nodded. "You can use the room where I've got all my sewing stuff. We can put some of that away. And use the bathroom next to it. I think it's all set with soap and shampoo, and there are towels in the hall closet."

"Okay. But won't Grandma be able to go home today?"

"She'll probably leave the hospital, but until they catch Dave Hillman, you'll all be safer here in town with us."

"They didn't get him last night?"

"No. Not yet." Kevin dished the eggs out onto three plates, leaving some for Tommy in the pan.

They ate in silence.

Annie finished first. "Those were good, thanks. Where's my backpack with my clothes?"

"You left it by the front door last night." Janet smiled as Annie left the room.

She's remarkable, remembering to be polite when they've been through so much the last week.

Annie shrieked.

Kevin was up and at the front of the house in seconds, Janet right behind him.

"We never had our video chat with Mom last night! We do that every night. I lost my cellphone so we used Grandma's Monday."

"I didn't see Cathy's phone with her things at the hospital," said Kevin.

Janet put a calming hand on Annie's shoulder. "Do you know the number? We could call from mine."

Annie shook her head. "It's saved on my phone. And we do it the same time every night, so it's early morning for her, I think. We don't want to call when she's asleep or at work. But she's going to be so worried.""

Kevin held up a calming hand. "You know her email?"

"Sure."

Janet opened email and handed her phone to Annie. "Put in her address. While you shower, I'll write her a note explaining why you missed the chat last night and I'll give her my number... Kevin, why don't you get Tommy up?"

"I'm up," said Tommy from behind them.

"Good. There are eggs waiting for you in the kitchen." Kevin steered Tommy out of the room.

Annie handed the phone back to Janet. "That's it. Tell Mom we love her."

"I will."

The Fat Envelope

Rob sat in his kitchen, staring at the contents of the fat envelope. The letter was dated July sixth. Henry died the fifteenth, but the envelope was postmarked a week later. *Who mailed it? Probably the same person who mailed the one to the pastor.*

It was several pages long, and there was a photo of Henry and Dave in 'Nam. *Probably when they first got there—so young and innocent.*

Rob began reading the letter.

July 6, 2022

Dear Rob,

I'm so sorry for all the things I said to you back in the day. You were right. The war was awful and stupid. Maybe every war is awful and stupid. I know you had it rough as a medic—I'm just glad you made it back alive.

I've never talked to anyone about what happened over there because I didn't want to remember. I wanted to pretend none of it was real. But I did things that are coming back to haunt me now, and I'm afraid. For myself and for Cathy, too. If anything happens to me, please look out for her.

Rob got up to refill his coffee, then went on to the next page.

Dave never should have enlisted. He was so scared. He depended on me. Then I got malaria and he was on his own for weeks. When I came back, he was jittery even in camp, not trusting anyone except me. He acted weird around the new sergeant, keeping his head down, avoiding him.

Six of us went out. We were in deep, all of us jumpy as hell, when we came under sniper fire. The gook got two of us before I managed to work around and take him out. It was the closest I'd ever been to a kill. I threw up before I went back to the squad.

That left me, Dave, this new kid from Texas, and the sergeant. We came on a deserted village. Dave was crazy jittery as we searched for V.C. Then the kid from Texas found a girl hiding. She was maybe twelve, maybe not even.

The sergeant rapes her. When he's done, he shoves Dave at her. Dave's so scared, I don't think he could actually do anything, but he goes through the motions.

Tears started to flow as Rob read, hearing Henry's voice.

Then the sarge pushes me at her. When I balk, he starts screaming at me, and the next thing I know, I've shot him dead. We high tail it out of there, the three of us. We don't even grab the sergeant's dog tags. We leave the girl lying there, curled up, and run.

The new kid keeps blathering on about how I'll be court-martialed until I can't take it anymore and I shoot him too. Dave stands there looking at me. Takes his dog tags off, gets the kid's, hands them to me. His eyes are wide and crazy scared—of me. "I stepped on a mine," he says. And he walks away. I don't even try to stop him. The sergeant goes down as MIA, Dave and the kid as KIA. The other two end up MIA, too, because we'd left their tags with the sarge.

Rob got up and walked to the sink, holding it while he sobbed, letting the tears flow freely. When they slowed, he took a deep breath, rinsed his face, dried it off with a paper towel, and blew his nose. He went back to finish the letter.

I extend my tour, trying to make up for what I did, trying to find Dave. I don't know what I'll do if I find him. Then I spot him in Saigon when I'm waiting to ship out the last time. Only I'm not sure. I follow him, taking pictures while he goes around collecting money from people. When he takes out a gun and shoves it in a guy's gut, I snap a photo of that, too. I stop breathing when he pulls the trigger. He pulls money out of the guy's wallet, takes a watch off his wrist, and walks away cool as can be.

The next day, I leave the camera behind. I've gotta talk to him to believe it's really Dave. It is. He's hard. Tells me to let him stay dead, not tell anyone he's alive. Tells me the V. C. had him for months, tortured him, then drug runners came into the village where he was being held and they took him. Thought they could trade him, but somehow he ended up working with them instead.

I counted myself lucky to walk away from him that day. When I got home, I got those pictures developed and put them in an envelope in a safety deposit box. I figured they'd balance our secrets, if he ever came back.

He's back now. I don't think money's all he wants. If you get this, I'm dead. Please, protect Cathy. We've had a good marriage and we love each other, but I know how hard it was for you at our wedding and I know she loved you first. I don't think she stopped caring about you. Please Rob, take care of her.

Rob put the letter down, and picked up a photo of the two young men who went to war. Rob stretched his neck. He sat back and stared at the pages before him. *Cathy never got to read Henry's letter for her. She doesn't need every detail, but she deserves the truth.*

He shoved it all back into the envelope. He'd wait until Cathy was feeling better to read parts to her.

At the Hospital

Cathy had been cleared to go home, but Janet's phone rang with a call from Tina. After she'd heard an abbreviated version of the previous day's events and been assured they were all staying in town with Janet until the man was caught, Tina asked Janet to set up a video chat. "It's late here and I'll rest better seeing Mom and the kids."

"Of course."

When they'd visited a few minutes Tina asked to speak to Cathy privately.

Once they closed the door, Cathy addressed her daughter. "Okay, it's just us. What do we have to discuss in private, Tina?"

"I know the original plan was for me to pick up the kids and go back to our old house, but that's hours away from you. With Dad gone, would you want us to move in with you? I'd feel better knowing you aren't out in the sticks all alone. I'll be working remotely, so that's not a problem."

"How would the kids feel about moving and changing schools? Annie won't miss her friends?"

"Most of her friends' parents were our friends as a couple. After the divorce, I got dropped socially. Annie didn't tell me right away, but apparently she felt her friends distancing themselves, too. She definitely wants to move. And they love it there."

Cathy paused to choose her words. "Truthfully? As much as I've enjoyed having the kids here, I'm afraid I'd end up in a parenting role, living together all the time. Grandparenting is more fun. But you know what? I like having a garden, but I don't need that big orchard. If I move into town, would you want the farm?"

"Of course, but are you sure?"

"It would make sense for you to move in when you get back, so the kids can start school here. I wouldn't have to rush into a new place."

"Okay. Maybe Janet would want you to move in with her."

"Maybe." Cathy wasn't going to rush into anything with Rob, but Tina was sure to recognize the feelings between them. *I hope it won't upset her.*

The Hillmans and Edna Johnson

"I will not help a murderer." Steve was heading for the front door to alert the deputy across the street when Dave came down the stairs.

"Where do you think you're going?" barked their mother. "You need to get your brother out of here."

Steve turned to look at the two of them.

There was a hard glisten to both sets of eyes watching him.

His Beretta was clenched in his hand, hanging by his side. He slid the safety off.

What the hell am I doing? This is my family.

"He killed Henry Clark." Steve tried one more time to get through to his mother.

"No, he didn't. I did that," claimed the old woman. "I fixed the brakes on his car, and Janet's too. I borrowed an automotive repair book from the library. It's really not that difficult, except for getting back up off the pavement. I did have to use vice grips. My hand strength's not what it used to be."

Steve stared at her in shock. "You're ninety-two years old. You're lying. He did it."

"Fine. Don't believe me." She shrugged both shoulders as if it didn't matter. "Henry told you about your brother. It was only a matter of time before he told someone else. And Janet saw Davey. And of course he had to get that envelope away from Cathy Clark."

Steve switched his gaze to his brother. "Were you really going to burn that house with the children in it?"

Dave shrugged. "Do you remember me in high school? Do you remember what I wanted to be?"

Steve shook his head. "You never talked much."

"Yeah. I don't remember, either. But what I am? That's thanks to Henry Clark. That evidence he had? Photos, from

Saigon, fifty years ago. It's not even the same country anymore. No one would care. I'm not hiding what I am from anyone. Henry didn't understand that, because he was hiding a lot from everyone. It was fun to see him terrified... I was going to burn the house down before he died, with everyone except Henry in it. Destroy his life."

"But he was already dead. You say he couldn't hurt you... why go after the kids?"

Dave tilted his head and grimaced. "It wasn't fair that Henry had everything, when it was his fault I've had no life. I wanted to destroy what he'd had." Dave looked Steve in the eye. "Honestly, I didn't realize the kids were there, though it probably wouldn't have made a difference..." He nodded at the gun in his little brother's hand. "You're not going to use that. But I'll tell you what. Get me out of here today and I'll stay away, I'll just tell you where to send money when I need it. We'll let everyone think I killed Henry and slipped away on my own. After all, I've been a ghost most of my life. That won't be a hard sell."

Let everyone think I killed Henry? Steve was confused. His brother acted like a killer—it was clear he would have burned down that house with or without the kids in it—but their mother claimed she was the one who killed Henry. Steve tried to imagine her down on the ground with her vice grips, reaching under the car to open a bleeding nipple on the brake.

Could she really have done that? Is Dave really covering for her?

Seeing his little brother's confusion, Dave stepped toward Steve with confidence. "I'll take the gun."

"No." Steve brought the weapon up to firing level.

Dave grinned and plunged toward him. Steve fired, hitting his brother point blank in the center of his chest. Dave grabbed the weapon and fought for it. Steve's finger pulled the trigger again. This time the bullet went up through Dave's chin and he collapsed.

Their mother shrieked and fell on his body, shaking his lifeless shoulders.

Steve let the gun fall to the floor. He turned and walked toward the front door. He didn't recognize the click for what it was until the first bullet hit him. They kept coming until he collapsed.

The sheriff's deputy came running in, saw the two bodies on the floor, then watched in helpless horror as Mrs. Hillman put the weapon under her chin and pulled the trigger.

The deputy called for medical assistance as he rushed outside to vomit in the bushes by the front door. When he stopped retching, he went back to check for a pulse on Steve Hillman. By then there was none. There was no reason to check the others. There was little left of their heads.

The deputy was rinsing out his mouth in the kitchen sink and didn't hear the light tap on the front door.

Everyone knew the sheriff was looking for David Hillman, who'd been presumed dead for decades. Edna Johnson had come to offer her sympathy to his mother and get more details.

She'd often heard interesting things by entering an open door after a light tap—not loud enough to be heard, but enough to say she *had* knocked.

Edna saw Steve's body and ran to him, not seeing the blood at first. Then she saw the others. With a small scream she crumpled to the floor in a faint.

The ambulance attendants quickly established they had only one live patient, and all she needed was smelling salts.

Beginnings

Sunday, July 9, 2023

Cathy tugged at one last flower and stood to look at Henry's grave. She was finally satisfied with the arrangement.

"We love you." She always said those words aloud.

When Rob had finally let her read the entire letter that Henry had sent to him, she'd spent hours here, hoping Henry's spirit could somehow sense her understanding of what he did as a frightened teenager in a horrific place.

Cathy sighed, remembering how happy they'd been at the beginning of July a year ago, and how quickly he had changed, how frightened he'd been.

Sorry your last birthday with us wasn't better. We miss you, but I'm glad you're finally at peace.

So much had happened since then. Tina and the kids had moved in with Cathy. The kids liked their new school. They'd all adjusted to Cathy's friendship with Rob blooming back into the romantic relationship they'd had in high school. Janet and Kevin got married and traveled in Europe for two months before he moved in with her. They were planning their next big trip to Australia, New Zealand, and Southeast Asia. Cathy was going to stay at Janet's house while they were gone.

Life's good, Henry. Rob's taking care of me, like you told him to—but you know he would have anyway. We're scandalizing the gossips by holding hands in public.

Henry had never cared much for gossip. He'd get a kick out of that.

Cathy noticed Edna Johnson across the cemetery.

Edna Johnson has adopted the Hillmans – there's no family left. I see her out here tending to their graves. She was there that day, but she doesn't talk about it – believe it or not!

***

Rob stood on the knoll where he'd been the day Henry was buried. He watched while Cathy said goodbye again. Memories of Henry would always be with them, but his ghost was in their lives less and less each day. Rob walked down to join Cathy. He took her hand in his as he reached her side. She looked into his eyes and smiled.

They walked away. Together.

Resources

The Veterans Administration hosts the

PTSD: National Center for PTSD

https://www.ptsd.va.gov/

Veterans Crisis Line

800-273-8255 and Press 1

or

988 and Press 1

Anyone can dial 988 and Press 1, if they're worried about a
loved one who may need crisis support.

The Veterans Crisis Line is also available by chat at
VeteransCrisisLine.net/Chat and text **838255**

Thank you

Thank you for reading this book.

Please take a few moments right now, while the story is still resonating, to help others find it.

Amazon's algorithms control book sales – the more reviews and ratings a book gets, the more often it pops up for people to see. The more attention it gets there, the more attention it gets elsewhere and the more likely it will find its way to libraries, too.

So please, review this book on Amazon. You don't have to purchase it there to post a review and/or rate a book. You can copy and paste the same review at Goodreads or other places. A review can be short and simple – "Interesting story." is enough to be counted. Don't forget to give it a star rating.

If you want to do more, you can:

- Talk it up – encourage your friends and your local library or book club to get the book.

- If you do social media, post your picture with the book.

Every bit helps.

Thanks.

www.sherimcguinn.com/books
sherimcguinn.substack.com/

Also by Sheri McGuinn

Running Away: Maggie's Story

Maggie is already in another state when they realize she's gone. Her mother's missing journal is their only clue. While Peg races to find her daughter before she's hurt or disappears forever, Maggie finds herself in dangerous company. Told in both voices, this is a stand-alone story, yet companion to *Peg's Story: Detours*.

Peg's Story: Detours

A novel that reads like memoir; one woman's journey. Asked for by readers of *Running Away*, this is the full story of Maggie's mother.

Kirkus Reviews summarized it like this: "In some ways, the novel is a brutal cautionary tale, showing how one mistake can spiral into a life-changing series of events. In another, however, it is a moving coming-of-age narrative about a girl who discovers herself amid extreme circumstances. A nuanced yet plainly told novel."

Tough Times

"Stay together." Michael knows they'll be split up by the system, so he decides to take his young siblings to the white grandparents they've never known – because *his* father was black. While Michael deals with responsibility, grief, prejudice, fear, his first romantic relationship, and hormones, the police find his mother and label it murder. They think Michael did it, but the killer is stalking the kids.

2023 KINDLE BEST OF INDIE BOOK AWARDS FINALIST YOUNG ADULT

Alice

Thirteen-year-old Nina narrates the story of her mother, Alice, who has always been responsible, proper, and totally uptight. The school eliminates Alice's teaching position, then her hippie father drops into their lives, and then the bank sends a letter threatening their home – and Nina suddenly sees another side to her mother.

Behind the Story

My senior year of high school I was corresponding with Andy while he served a second tour in 'Nam as a Marine. Also during those months, the massacre at My Lai became public knowledge, and a month before I graduated, protesting students were gunned down by the National Guard at Kent State. Gap years were not a thing then, but I took one.

Vietnam loomed so large in our lives. We'd been brought up with movies glorifying the heroics of World War II and Hogan's Heroes making even a prison camp look like a day in the park. When the movie M*A*S*H came out in early 1970, it was based in Korea and, while it had plenty of humor on top, underneath was the gritty realism of a MASH unit trying to keep young soldiers alive.

When the Pentagon papers were published in June 1971, protests increased. In June 1972 the photo of the "Napalm Girl" was first published and public sentiment against the war solidified. We signed the Paris Peace Accords in January 1973 and by March 1973 the last American ground troops were pulled out of Vietnam. However, by the terms of the Accord, Americans were still able to provide logistical support to the Republic of Vietnam. Military personnel were limited to fifty, so most of that activity was staffed by civilian contractors.

Vietnam vets had never been greeted with enthusiasm. The public knew too much about the nastiness of war. Saigon fell in April 1975. On top of everything else, veterans had to deal with the fact that all their sacrifices had been for naught.

In 1981, I decided to write a book with characters dealing with the aftermath of that war that was never declared a war. I read a stack of books by veterans and others to understand my characters. That spring, I rented a Commodore 128 for a month and wrote the book. In May I flew to NYC for the ASJA conference. I got to hear Alex Haley and Mary Higgins Clark speak, and I took a workshop on pitching, then pitched my novel (a first draft) to real NYC agents!

My timing was right. The July 13, 1981 issue of Time Magazine would devote the Nation section to "The Forgotten Warriors."

Two of those NYC agents requested the novel. Back then, they asked for the whole thing rather than a few pages. So I printed out a copy on continuous feed paper and made photocopies to mail out. I got one form rejection and one that said he liked my writing but there were too many characters in this story. I didn't realize that meant I should call and ask how soon he wanted a revision. Besides, the computer had been returned and I didn't have anyone encouraging me to write. So I got busy with life.

I moved six times. Still, when I got my first paycheck for writing in 2005 and started writing seriously, that original paper copy with the perforated edges was still in a file box. I read it – and it had too many characters! I'd been trying to tell too many stories at once.

Running Away seemed more urgent. But *All for One* kept calling me. When I started revising it last year, it was still hard to get Vietnam vets to talk about 'Nam. So, instead of leaving the story in its original time, I decided to age my characters to reflect the lasting effect of war on those who fight and those who love them. It didn't have to be Vietnam; win or lose, war is never a glamorous endeavor. At its best, it is necessary.

I hope you enjoyed the story.

Acknowledgments

I've been writing all my life. While teachers always praised my work, I never had a mentor guide me toward publication. I still don't have one particular person, but I now have a network.

My children and their offspring bring balance and joy into my life. They've helped with ideas when I was stuck and I can always depend on them to give honest and useful feedback.

Multiple writing critique groups in California, Arizona, and Nevada have provided sound recommendations along the way. The Business of Writing group in Auburn, CA, is an ongoing source of support for all business decisions and creative ones as well. Heidi Struve Currey, Nicolle Goldman, Rebecca Inch-Partridge, and Joan Griffin have been particularly helpful this year.

Friends made through the California Film Arts Alliance continue to be good resources. Authors Guild and other memberships have also extended my network of support. Professionals like Hope Clark have paid for my writing. Victoria Lucas encourages my screenwriting.

People from the past have played key roles in my becoming a professional writer. Barbie Gorham Mahjoubi, if you see this please contact me. Searching for you after 9/11 led to Michael D. Sellers, who I'd met at your wedding. We hadn't seen each other in over twenty years, but he paid me to revise a screenplay – my first paycheck as a writer. He and another friend, John Jarchow, have connected me with other paid writing gigs.

For this story in particular, thank you to Chuck Jones, who explained how to sabotage the car. Thank you to all the vets who wrote firsthand accounts of their experiences. Thank you

Donald Dykstra, John Asbury and Dennis Wiley, Vietnam vets in Riverview who responded to my pleas for information on how enlistment worked back then. And a special thank you to Andy, whose letters from 'Nam survived even more moves than the original manuscript of this book. Henry is not you, but your letters helped me find his teenage voice.

Thank you all, and everyone I missed, too.

Thanks. Sheri

5/26/2025

Discussion Questions

1. Can you understand or forgive Henry's secret? Do you have any empathy for "the bad man"? What are the implications in real life?

2. Everyone assumes Henry is being paranoid and/or his PTSD is returning. Do we make that kind of assumption whenever someone has a diagnosis?

3. Rob was the leader with "all for one" - then he did not stick with them. He says he became a medic to save lives. Did he betray the friendship? Was guilt part of the reason for his post-service choices?

4. Mrs. Hillman mentions growing up in WWII Europe. What impact do you think that had on her understanding of her Davey going to war, going AWOL, coming back so changed? Do you think she's had contact with her Davey before this?

5. Consider the opening scenes in 2022. How would you describe Cathy's feelings toward her husband? Does she love him? Has she loved Rob all along?

6. Janet wanted a life of adventure, but came home to take care of her parents when they were disabled. Are you happy for her at the end?

7. Who did kill Henry?

My website has:

Supplemental Materials

Puchasing Links

A Contact Form (ask questions or set up an author visit)

Media Resources

www.sherimcguinn.com

My newsletter caters to readers and writers:

https://sherimcguinn.substack.com/

Review links for *All for One: Love, War, & Ghosts*:

www.amazon.com/dp/B0FG28Z761

www.goodreads.com/book/show/235247041

Every review helps – thank you.

Thanks for reading!

www.ingramcontent.com/pod-product-compliance
Lightning Source LLC
Chambersburg PA
CBHW020417180626
46812CB00003B/1027